THE PROFESSOR

SKYE WARREN

"Never let formal education get in the way of your learning."

—Mark Twain

CHAPTER ONE

Sweet and Full-bodied

"**T**HIS DRESS IS too short," I say, tugging at the hem. It reveals too much of my thighs, making it hard to walk without flashing everyone. The material is stretchy but not enough. When I pull from the bottom, it drags down the top, making the neckline even lower.

"That's the point," Daisy says.

She's my best friend, roommate, and the leader of this particular escapade. She also has the body of a runway model, which means this slinky, barely there little black dress looks classy on her. It looks like it belongs in this lobby with its marble floors, chandeliers, and velvet seating.

Instead of garish, the way it looks on me.

Usually my clothes attempt to hide my large bust.

Then again, nothing about this evening is

usual.

I tug the V-neck up, which threatens to show everyone my black panties.

"Focus, Anne," she says. "If we play this right, you can stop worrying about money."

"I only need two hundred for that one economics textbook that isn't available used. Oh, and some of those essay exam notebooks they make us buy."

"You're asking for five hundred dollars. Not a penny less."

Five hundred dollars. What would a man do to me for that much money? "What about half the money for half the time?"

She shakes her head, making her curls bounce against her rouged cheek. "Five hundred dollars for one hour is the minimum. That's why we paid for the Uber to get this far away from campus, where people actually have money."

"And where no one will recognize us."

She giggles. "No one would recognize you right now."

That's probably true. Anne Hill wears jeans from Goodwill. Between my wardrobe change and the fake lashes that Daisy put across my eyelids, I look like a stranger in the reflection of the thick brass railings that decorate the space.

We make our way up a small staircase to the floating bar area, which hums with conversation. It's filled with older men who look like they've probably already experienced a wealthy midlife crisis and own five Lamborghinis. There are a handful of women, but they look older, too. Sophisticated. They look like they belong in this thousand-dollar-a-night hotel.

Daisy grabs a seat at the bar, easily hopping onto the high leather stool.

I follow more gingerly as I negotiate my way up without disturbing the sanctity of the dress. "But if I charge more, won't he expect more? Won't he expect…experience?"

She rolls her eyes. "First day of school is in one week, and you know what that means? That means a bunch of syllabuses, with even more textbook and supply requirements."

"Syllabi," I say absently.

"Okay, English lit major. You also get those supplementary materials."

"Most of those are at the university library." She's an engineering major, and in keeping with their technology focus, most of their textbooks have gone online. You can rent them for a semester. In deference to tradition, the humanities department continues to deal in mostly paper textbooks. Huge, expensive textbooks that change slightly every year so that we have to buy new ones.

"I mean I guess you could blow your professor for a copy, but considering he also gets royalties as the author, it feels like you're paying him twice."

"Daisy!" She came from a super strict cult-like community, but she hasn't cut ties. She has no problem going home, wearing linen dresses down to her ankles and smiling with those baby-blue eyes. Then she returns to college, swears like a sailor.

And drinks like one too.

The bartender appears wearing a white dress shirt and suspenders in keeping with the old-world grandeur of the Pinnacle Hotel. It was built in the nineteen twenties, and even though they must have renovated in order to keep things looking so beautiful, the design has remained the same. This is what it must have felt like as a glamorous flapper girl.

A glamorous flapper girl in desperate need of money, that is.

"What can I get you?" he asks with a mega-watt smile.

"Nothing," Daisy says, grinning. "But if someone sends us drinks, we want them."

A wink. "You got it."

"Do you think he knows?" I whisper as he walks away.

She shrugs. "Does it matter? Everyone uses sex for something."

"Love? Pleasure?"

"This isn't a fairy tale. And unless you want to be back here every week, I suggest you stand your ground. They're going to ask for the night, but you only give them an hour. That way if they want longer, they have to pony up another five hundred."

"One thousand dollars." More money than I've ever held in my hands.

"They'll try to negotiate you down, of course. Do not under any circumstance go lower than two hundred an hour. I'm serious about that."

"Do people even carry that kind of cash?"

"Of course they do. For rich people that's like ten dollars."

"I feel like most places don't even take cash these days."

"Well, you can always take Venmo."

I shiver. "And leave a paper trail?"

"The federal government doesn't care what you're doing, babe. Though if you're nervous, you can always send him downstairs to get cash from the concierge. He definitely wouldn't be the first guy with a raging hard-on to do it."

"Oh God."

"If he leaves you alone in the room, be sure to raid the minibar. Little bottles work great in your backpack between classes."

"Tell me you aren't serious."

"Trust me. Chemical engineering is so much easier to understand when you're buzzed."

Daisy and I don't have much in common, really. Except the fact that we're both full-ride scholarship students who live in the most broken-down dorm at Tanglewood University. We were paired as roommates and have stuck together ever since. We're both relatively neat, focused on our education, and most importantly, don't get drunk and pee on the carpet like my friend Allison's first roommate did.

"Well," she says, drawing out the word. "You can always ask Aaron."

I make a face. "Absolutely not."

"Come on, he's hot. In a frat-boy kind of way."

"He's...cute." He's more than cute. He's the cool kid on campus. The one every girl wants to be with, and every boy wants to be friends with. And at one point, he seemed interested in me. He asked me out to a keg party, but when I wouldn't drink enough warm frothy beer to go upstairs to a bedroom to have sex, he sent me home in an Uber.

And I found out later, he banged someone else.

"More importantly, he's loaded. He could swipe his daddy's credit card for a few thousand bucks, and no one would even notice."

"We aren't even really dating. Everyone talks about his endless hookups."

"I'm not suggesting you marry the guy. Just let him buy you stuff."

"And then have sex with him?"

"Most likely."

"Well, if I'm going to have sex with someone for money, I'd rather it be a stranger. Not someone I have to see every day on campus."

"Great, because here comes a guy. Remember to smile, giggle, and shake your tits."

"Oh God."

"Just pretend he's one of those old poems you love so much. Then you'll be fascinated."

A man old enough to be our grandfather approaches us, his hair white, his suit austere, his eyes hungrily assessing. "Good evening, ladies. You're looking ravishing."

"Thank you so much," Daisy says, practically purring. "Lovely to meet you."

"Can I get you a drink?"

"Whiskey," she says. "Neat. I'm dying of thirst."

He raises a bushy gray eyebrow at me. "And you?"

"Water, thanks."

Daisy gives me a warning look. "Are you sure?"

"I'll…have the same. Whiskey." What did she call it? "Tidy."

An awkward silence ripples between us. Daisy laughs to clear it. "We've just come in from out of town and my friend here has jet lag."

"Poor thing," he says, not looking sympathetic at all. In fact, he's not looking at my face. He's staring at my breasts as if I'm an object for sale. Which I guess I am.

My skin crawls. "That's me. Super tired. I might need to go to bed early."

"Don't be silly," Daisy says with a pointed glance. "We're going to have so much fun tonight." The emphasis on the word *fun* brings an image of that economics textbook to mind. How else am I supposed to get two hundred dollars by next week?

"Fun, eh?" the man says. "I love a good time. The name's Saul."

Jesus. Has there even been a Saul born in the last century?

"Well, Saul, you look like a man who knows how to enjoy himself." Daisy gives him this playful jab on his arm that he takes as permission to stand close to her, close enough that she has to look up at him. Her eyes shine like she's actually enjoying herself, which is…painful.

Our drinks arrive and are promptly delivered. The man pays with a hundred-dollar bill, which is an insane amount of money for two drinks. A surreptitious glance at the thickness of the wallet shows that there are many more where that came from, thus proving Daisy's point. These people are loaded. Shame runs over me like lava.

The amber liquid shivers in the chandelier light.

"Delicious," Daisy says, taking a sip of the whiskey. "Sweet and full-bodied. Like my friend here. Now if it were tart and smoky, that would be me."

Saul licks his thin lips in appreciation. "I love a woman who can appreciate whiskey."

He runs an age-spotted hand over her lower back, dipping down to curve over her ass.

I've spent so many days wondering if I would be willing to do this.

I didn't even think about whether I actually *could*.

Despite Saul's interest in my breasts, he's clearly far more interested in Daisy's enthusiasm. Can I work up that kind of bubbly flirtation for someone three times my age?

She whispers something in his ear, and he smiles, revealing a row of super white teeth. Veneers, my mind supplies. He murmurs something back in her ear, and she giggles.

"We're going upstairs," she informs me.

"Great," I say, feeling grim.

"I'll book a room," he says before heading to the lobby.

"You can come with us," she whispers. "I bet he'll agree to both of us."

"Both of us?"

"Why have one for the price of one when you can get two for the price of two?"

"You're quoting the movie *Contact* at a time like this?"

"It's never not quotable. Jodie Foster is mother."

"I don't think I can do this."

"You're right. A threesome is too much for

your first time."

"That's not what I—"

"Remember what I told you. Five hundred dollars for an hour, not a penny less. If he ends up wanting ten hours, he pays ten times the amount."

"*Ten hours*?" What the hell could someone do to me in ten hours?

She's already gone, doing a little coquettish run to meet Saul at a bank of gold-plated, art deco elevators with old-fashioned cages as doors. They're already plastered to the wall, bodies pressed together in a mash that's supposed to represent sensuality by the time it ascends.

There's no way I can go through with this.

I'm grateful to Daisy for trying to help me, and Lord knows I need the money, but there's just no way I can go upstairs with a man like Saul.

Which means I'll have to spend money I don't have to catch a cab back to the dorms.

Shit.

The least I deserve is a sip of this expensive whiskey.

My very first sip of whiskey.

I study the glass. How does a liquid, *any* liquid, get to cost that much?

Do they infuse it with gold?

I take a sip, feeling it cool on my tongue.

Immediately followed by a burn.

A cough overtakes me. Another. And then a painful sputter.

She called this sweet? It's pure castor oil.

I probably look like an idiot in a room full of experienced drinkers.

Lovely. Well, what's a little humiliation to add to a night already so full of it?

"I wouldn't drink that either," comes a low masculine murmur.

CHAPTER TWO

Rare Books

I WHIRL, MY eyes still pricked with tears. I'm half expecting to see someone much older than Saul. Someone decrepit. Someone out of nightmares.

Instead I'm facing the most handsome man I've ever seen.

A strong brow shadows luminous, dark-coffee-colored eyes. His nose reminds me of a bust of some ancient Greek philosopher. Sensual lips curve in a secret smile, one we share out of our mutual distaste for whatever this is. He stands far enough back that I don't feel crowded against the bar, but somehow I still feel the heat emanating from his large body.

"How do people drink that?" I manage to say, my voice hoarse.

"If you're going to drink whiskey," he says,

"drink whiskey."

I blink. "Meaning?"

"Meaning that stuff's cheap."

"It was forty-five dollars," I say, defensive of Saul's ordering decisions.

He doesn't respond except to lift his hand. The bartender immediately drops what he's doing and hustles over. "A glass of Macallan 30 Sherry Oak."

It's poured right in front of me, the bottle fancy and heavy-looking.

"Salut," the bartender says before disappearing.

I study the liquid, which is a little darker but otherwise much the same.

"Trust me," the man in the suit says.

"I don't even know you."

"Exactly. What reason would I have to lie to you?"

A snort escapes me, even though the man has a point. What motive does he have for buying me what must be a ridiculously expensive drink just to show me that whiskey can taste good? I have to at least try it. And I suppose I'm a little curious. Could anything, even a more expensive barrel or different variety of grain, make it not taste like car oil?

The man leans forward, giving me a faint whiff of sandalwood and luxurious maleness. He isn't nearly as old as Saul, but he isn't as young as me either. Instead of being a turnoff, his age makes him seem confident, secure. Alluring.

"Take a deep breath," he says. "Hold it while you drink. And then breathe out through your mouth. It's the oxygen that makes it burn."

What the hell. I throw back a gulp, half expecting to cough up a storm onto the pristine bar top. Instead it goes down smooth. My eyes widen. There's almost a buttery aftertaste. A pleasant warmth lines my throat. "What the hell was *that*?"

Sensual lips curve. "Describe it to me. I want to know what your first time feels like."

Damn. That's presumptuous. And oddly attractive. I lick my lips. "It's smooth."

His lids lower. Those dark eyes focus on my mouth. "Yes."

The final note hums on my tongue. "And a little sweet. I didn't expect that."

"Whiskey can be sweet," he says, though it doesn't sound like he's talking about alcohol, not with that gravel in his voice, with the flames in his eyes. "There are hints of caramel in this one."

"Caramel." I run my finger along the thick-cut crystal embracing the whiskey.

"There are smoky ones. Floral. Buttery. I like the earthiness of a malt, personally."

"Malt?"

"I like to pretend I'm living in a remote cabin on a broad green slope, eating a hearty stew as I watch over my sheep."

I can't help the laugh. This man in a three-piece suit? "You are the furthest thing from a sheep farmer that I've ever seen."

He puts a hand on his chest. "Wounded. Then what am I?"

"Something that pays well, since you know that much about expensive whiskey."

"I see." He's waiting for more, his eyes challenging.

I study him. His handkerchief square is the same red as his tie. "Something...dignified. Something serious." But he dreams about living in a remote cabin in Ireland. Perhaps there's a hint of an artist in him. "Let's say...you're a rare book dealer. The successful kind."

He grins. "You could say that."

My stomach flutters. Is this what flirting between grown-ups is like? I mean, I've dated before. You don't get to be a junior at Tanglewood University without getting asked out by finance frat boys and theater majors alike. They take me to play pool at the rec center. Or occasionally an off-campus sports bar for wings and watered-down drinks. The night inevitably ends with the guy trying to get into my dorm room.

Daisy is my convenient excuse to keep them out.

Along with seven-thirty a.m. class times.

"How close was I?" I ask, wondering what this man really does. Probably not anything as interesting as rare books. That's just a fantasy of a bookworm like me. He probably does investment banking or fracking or some other calculating, extractive thing.

"My turn," he says, not answering.

I raise one eyebrow to express my doubt. I'm wearing Daisy's dress, which is the only even remotely interesting thing about my person. Otherwise I have brown hair—the color of a mouse, basically—wrapped into a fancy-looking ponytail. Brown eyes. A straight nose. Pink lips. The only compliment I've ever been paid is for my brain. She's so smart. So much potential. If only, if only. I like my brain, but it would be nice, especially in a world more interested in how women look, to have been called pretty once or twice.

"Go ahead," I say, my tone gentle, because there's nothing he can see.

His dark eyes narrow as he studies me from the boring crown of my head down to boring toes encased in someone else's shoes. "You don't belong here."

I stiffen. "What?"

"Oh, you're holding your poise quite well, of course. Admirably, but anyone can see that you're too fine for this place. Too much quality."

"Are you high? This place is maximum fancy."

A snort. "I'm here for a charity event that costs two thousand dollars a plate. There will be speeches, a silent auction, dancing—the entire thing will probably spend far more than it makes. Everyone smiling and laughing and drunk, and here you are, not belonging for a single second. You aren't shallow or hypocritical. You're refreshingly...you."

My nose scrunches. "Somehow you've made *not* belonging sound like a compliment. Which is impressive, but I've wanted to belong all my life."

A half smile. "I know, dear heart. Because you're unbearably earnest."

Dear heart? The tender, unlikely sobriquet makes me smile. "I'm...unbearable?"

He leans close, his breath warm against my

temple. "You make me want to run my tongue along the side of your neck to see if you taste sweet. In public. Without even asking your permission. I find the absence of your taste unbearable."

My breath catches. "You're a flirt."

He chuckles.

"And you're stalling."

"You doubt me, but I've been reading you like a book. Your hair, your ears, and God, your eyes. The absolute novels written in your eyes. Though I think the most telling points are your hands. Your fingers, to be precise."

I look at my ordinary hands wrapped around the expensive crystal. "Explain."

He nudges my finger away, revealing...nothing. More clear crystal. "You see? Ah, you don't." He presses his own finger where mine had been and pulls it away, revealing...the faint imprint of his fingerprint—small topographical lines whispered onto the glass. "This bar is full of those fingerprints...except for yours. Which means that you either shaved yours off because you're in the mob during the Prohibition era or you spent far too long with your hands in harsh chemicals. Most likely cleaning supplies."

I stare at him, dumbfounded and more than a

little horrified. It's supposed to be my deep dark secret, the way I scrubbed my parents' house from top to bottom with bleach before I moved into the dorm. How did a stranger figure it out in a matter of minutes?

"So I must conclude," he says, his voice lazy with satisfaction, "that you are Cinderella."

A borrowed dress from a roommate fairy godmother. An unlikely flirtation with a modern-day rich guy. And a ticking clock running out on our encounter.

My voice comes out low through the knot in my throat. "You could say that."

"Don't worry," he says, almost tender. "You'll be home before midnight."

I'm still looking at him with wide eyes, breathing hard. How was this so intimate?

"Tell me your name." It's stated like a request, but his tone is coaxing.

It makes me wonder what else he could coax me to do. "Anne," I say, because my name is common enough. It's also more authentic than giving him some fake stripper name like Bunny or Chastity. This doesn't feel like a fake stripper situation.

I don't want it to end, this moment of feeling flirty and playful.

This moment of feeling like an adult.

He leans close to me, close enough that I can see the blue flecks in his eyes. "Listen, Anne. I want you. And I'd really like to take you upstairs."

Oh God, he smells good. And he's handsome. This is how it would feel to have a grown man proposition you. It's mature and sophisticated and—

"But before I do," he murmurs, "I want to make a few things clear."

I blink in confusion. "Like what?"

"One hour only."

My stomach sinks. This wasn't grown up. This wasn't flirting. It was the prelude to a transaction, even if it didn't feel as skeevy as it did with Saul. "That's my line."

"And I like to play games."

A shiver runs over my skin. "I'm guessing you don't mean crossword puzzles."

His soft exhale has amusement—but even more than that, leashed desire. "I enjoy the *New York Times* on Sunday as much as anyone, but that's not what I had in mind."

I'm almost afraid to ask. "Then what kind of games do you mean?"

"I want you to beg. To moan. To whimper. I might even make you cry, but I promise not to leave a mark. Name your price…Anne."

My cheeks turn scarlet. He's offering money for sex. Even though that's why I came here, the reality of sitting in this moment, having a man negotiate for my body sets me aflame. The way he says my name tells me he suspects it's a fake, an irony that makes me flinch.

A dark eyebrow rises. "Did I misread the situation?"

I clear my throat. "No. You nailed it, except for one part."

"What's that?"

"You won't make me cry." Nothing does. I haven't cried in years. Eons.

His eyes glint with pleasure. "Then tell me what it's going to take to bring you upstairs."

It's going to take pretending I'm a different woman, that my dress isn't so short, and that a man like you might want a girl like me for more than a freaking hourly rate. *You can't do this.* Then again, how can I afford not to? That damn economics textbook lands with a thud.

"One thousand dollars," I blurt out.

A slow smile spreads. "I have a feeling you'll be worth it."

Oh shit. I'm actually doing this. My body feels itchy in this dress. It seems to have shrunk two sizes when I stand up, my breasts pushing up, my thighs on display.

He's all gentlemanly manners as he helps me on my wobbly heels. No leering at my tits like Saul. No groping my ass, even though he already paid for the right. We leave the hotel bar as demurely as any regular couple going upstairs to fuck.

He pauses at the front desk to get a room.

I shiver beneath the glittering chandeliers. *You don't belong here.*

Then he's back, putting his coat around me. It's intimate, being surrounded by his warmth— everywhere. Catching the spice and masculine scent of him.

A hand at the base of my back leads me to the elevator.

Aged mirrors set in crown molded wood reflect my voluptuous body and cat eyes back to me. I only have a second to see that stranger before he pushes me back and kisses me. I'm leaned back over the large brass railing, off-center, completely reliant on him for my balance.

My hands clench in his shirt.

He kisses me as if he's about to go to war. As if he wants to remember the taste.

I push back, panting. "What's your name?"

His hand cups my jaw, turning me, tilting me, kissing me again until I'm exposed to him. Plundered. Used. We're both breathing hard when he breaks away. I'm lost in a sea of sensual uncertainty, waves splashing like cold froth against heated skin.

He rests his forehead against mine. "Will. But you'll call me sir."

Will. Is that his real name? Or fake? I gave him my real name, but he still could have given me a false one. I didn't realize how empty it would feel to not know who someone really is when you're in their arms. In a way calling him *sir* could be easier.

More anonymous.

"Is this part of the game?"

"It's very real. Tonight you're mine."

CHAPTER THREE

Every Goddamn Cent

A DING BREAKS the spell, and he pulls away from me. The elevator car jostles us a little, as if a completely smooth ride would degrade the historical accuracy. Metal rattles as he pulls the gate open, gesturing for me to proceed with him.

It's not a hallway that I step into.

It's a suite.

A ridiculously large, luxurious suite. I walk through the large canvases of art deco paintings and leather-and-brass furniture as carefully as if I'm in a museum. I'm drawn to the windows encased in thick, brocaded wood. Framed art of the city itself.

The cab that picked us up outside the dorm took us to Cressida City, a small upscale town on the outskirts of Tanglewood. Just enough room for grand houses and golf courses, the occasional theater. More wealth in a few square miles than there is in the entire urban sprawl.

From the window I can see the jagged lines of downtown.

And distantly, beyond that, is the university.

He comes up behind me. I feel his warmth, scent his allure. Will or whoever he is puts his arms around me from behind. He rests his cheek against my hair. "Beautiful, isn't it?"

"Yes." I scan the horizon, but when I meet his gaze in the window, he's not looking at the skyline. He's looking at me. My cheeks turn warm. I shift in his arms, looking for space, for distance, for safety, but somehow I only end up pinned to the wall between windows.

His palms hold the disparate window frames on either side of me, body leaned close, eyes dark with only the stars to illuminate him. It's a prison, one made of strong, good-smelling male instead of iron bars. A prison that feels far too good. An illusion. A trick of the light.

"Six letters," he says, drawing his hand up my arm, making goose bumps rise. His lids lower as his gaze sweeps down the length of me, to the too-tall shoes I borrowed. "Six letters that describe your body. Any guesses?"

He wants to play crossword puzzles after all.

"Boring."

He shakes his head, not breaking eye contact. "Try again."

It's hard to breathe beneath his intense regard. "Chubby."

"Erotic."

"The *New York Times* would never."

His lips curve. "Lovely."

"Maybe."

"Edenic." It means idyllic or pure.

Shit. "I like a man with a large vocabulary."

"Savory. Carnal. Or how about this one: un-fucking-real."

He thinks my body is unreal. "That's too many letters when you—"

He puts his mouth against mine, and I can't talk anymore, can't tell him it's too many letters when he puts the word *fucking* in the middle, but I suppose that's the point. It's the point as he consumes me, as he marauds me, as he uses that clever tongue to make me moan.

"I like that game," he says. "But I have another one."

A shiver runs through me. My nipples are hard, pressing against the slinky fabric of the dress without a bra to contain them. The room feels cold everywhere that Will isn't touching me.

Everywhere except my neck, where his large hand circles.

He squeezes gently, so gently, but the sensation makes me gasp. Only a millimeter of pressure on such a vulnerable place. It's enough to make my eyes roll back.

Something sweeps across my body. Heat. Electricity. Longing.

Is this what arousal feels like?

It's not how I thought it would be. Not anything like the wet, clumsy kisses I've experienced in frat houses and keg parties. This is firelight in feeling form. It races along my skin, from the faint pressure at my throat over my breasts, centering at the apex of my thighs.

It's a grown-up feeling, probably because I'm with a grown-up.

Even without his age, he feels more substantial than any boy who's ever kissed me. A man. One with faint scruff that rubs along my cheek as he presses close, as he kisses and bites his way across my jaw. One with muscles and stature and a thick erection pressing against my thigh. A very large erection, large like his vocabulary.

I like a man with a large vocabulary.

I can't believe I said that. Maybe I do know how to flirt. It just came out.

It was only the truth.

Then two fingers pinch my nipple through the dress, and I whimper.

I whimper the way he promised I would.

"Do you like that?" he murmurs.

"N-no," I say, my breath shuddering out.

"Little liar. If I put my fingers in your pussy, you'd be wet."

My sex clenches. This is so wrong. That I'm in some fancy hotel suite. That I'm being fondled by a stranger. And most of all, that he's right. I can feel the dampness between my thighs. More wetness than I've ever sensed before, even when I put my fingers between my legs in the middle of the night. If he touched me there, I would melt all over him.

"Please," I whisper.

"Please what? Please stop?"

A moan vibrates in my throat, and he must feel it. He must feel it against his pulse like a butterfly trying to break free even more than he hears it.

"Would you like me to please send you downstairs to the hotel bar all flushed and panting for everyone to see what I'm doing to you?"

"Oh God," I moan.

Even in the dim light, I can see the tilted

curve of his smile, a slice of moon in the night. It's evil, that smile. Devious. Knowing. "Everyone was already eye-fucking you when I picked you up." They were? I can't process that statement, because he keeps going. "Circling like a pack of fucking wolves around a lonely, stranded doe."

"No one..." I manage. "No one noticed me."

"Everyone wanted this pretty little body. So plump and sweet. So primed to bite."

"It isn't me," I say, panting as he tweaks my other nipple. It isn't me, I mean. It's the cat eyes. The dress. The glamorous setting. No one wants plain Anne Hill. Nothing special.

"Practically shivering with nerves. With fear," he says, almost snarling. "Do you know how dangerous that is to show to a man like me? How much I like it?"

Dangerous. His hand is wrapped around my neck. That's risky, isn't it? Especially for a man I never met before tonight. A man I might not even have his real name. Is this handsome stranger named Will? It's dangerous, yet somehow I feel safe in his grasp. Because the hand around my neck pins me down, marks me as his, because he claimed me before any of the other older men could. "Yes, sir," I whisper.

His eyes flash with sensual lightning. "Ah,

you've sealed your fate tonight, darling girl."

A shiver runs through me. "That sounds ominous."

He rests his forehead against mine. The hand that was around my neck moves behind it, cradling me, as if I'm precious. It's less sexual than before but somehow more intimate.

We're breathing the same air.

Becoming attuned through the air, which is somehow more prescient than words.

"I should put you in a cab and send you home," he murmurs.

"Don't," I say, because I need the thousand dollars. Though if I'm honest, that's not the complete reason why I want to stay. I want to see what it's like to be with a man who knows how to make my body sing. It's a melody I've never heard before.

Staying with him means knowing more about myself.

"I can't," he admits, his voice hoarse. "Too damned selfish."

"If you were selfish, you wouldn't have agreed to a thousand dollars."

A rough laugh. "Money is nothing compared to what you're giving me. Your body. Intimacy. Trust. You're going to earn every goddamn cent tonight."

Another shiver, but I raise my chin, defiant. "Because you'll make me cry?"

"Because I'm so fucking angry."

For the first time, I feel genuine fear. The kind that's primal, native to every woman, passed down from womb to womb, the innate knowledge of what can happen to her when she's alone in a room with a man.

CHAPTER FOUR

Higher Education

I'VE HAD FRIENDS who had posters of boy bands on their walls, of pop stars with pointy chins and puffs of hair on top. I can admire them in an abstract way. They are pleasing in the way a flower would be. This man, with his square jaw and hard-packed features? With his dark eyes, flashing with lightning? He doesn't belong in anything as static as a poster. He's only something my mind could have conjured, eyes closed, hands between my legs under the covers. I would be more afraid of him if I wasn't fascinated by the anger—anger I never let myself feel. Good girls should be quiet and studious and kind...and never, ever angry. I pushed it so far down that I hardly remember that I have it, at least until I feel the answering call to his anger.

"Angry at who?" I ask, breathless.

He pulls me close, his hand spread on my lower back, pressing us close. His lips are an inch from mine. "I'm angry at myself. For letting myself be dragged back to this godforsaken city, where I have to pretend like everything is fine, like I'm not walking through a battlefield."

Tanglewood is a large urban center with world-class museums and doctors and schools. The best humanity has to offer. It also has crime and poverty and desperation, the worst of humanity. Where does this man with his fancy suit and expensive whiskey land?

How can a man this wealthy and this confident be made to do anything?

He tugs down the neckline of my dress, revealing my breasts. My nipples look dark, flushed, and he runs his thumb over them until I exhale a sound of hunger.

He pulls back, the glint in his eyes slightly malevolent. "And I'm going to take it out on this delicious little body, going to make you squirm and writhe, going to listen to your whimpers like they're a bedtime lullaby."

The words shouldn't make me hot. They shouldn't.

He puts a hand in my hair, hair that's freshly washed and blown dry, that's been straightened and styled. He makes a mess of it, clenching it in his fist. It doesn't feel like a careless act. It's deliberate. As he tugs my head back, ever so slowly, I feel something contract inside me. A white-hot arousal. Some deep part of myself that wants to be dragged by a strong mate into a cave. I gasp at the sensation of pain and pleasure.

He gives a low laugh. "You like being man-handled."

I shiver.

"That's convenient," he continues, almost casually. Clenching that fist and releasing, tugging me around just to show he can. "Because that's what I intend to do to you."

It turns me liquid. It's not a conscious decision. I become this fluid thing.

He moves me like a doll, a plaything.

He drags me—that's the only word for it, drags—toward the far wall, the one overlooking the city. It's not fast, but impossibly slow. Enough time for me to resist, but I'm boneless, eyes almost rolling back, turned into quicksilver in his dominant fire.

My hands land on a carved windowsill, but instead of being backed against the wall like before, I'm facing the open window. There's a thin sash at the top, something that can be dropped down for privacy. It's open. I'm bared to the entire city.

Exposed.

Shame washes over me with only the smallest bite of pride.

This man chose me. He's putting me on display.

The affluent Cressida City doesn't have a bunch of skyscrapers like downtown Tanglewood, so I don't know if anyone can really see me three floors up. Would the people crossing the street in their fancy eveningwear look up? Is someone in the restaurant on the corner drinking wine to the view of my bared body?

He reaches around me, hands cupping my breasts, an offering for that invisible observer, tweaking the nipples so they're hard and pointing toward the window.

"A perfect handful," he murmurs, his voice vibrating against the side of my neck. He licks me there. Bites. Runs his teeth along the edge until I moan. "I'll be imagining these in my sleep, dreaming about your tits, mouth watering in the middle of the night to taste them."

Both of his hands reach down. They tug the too-short hem of the dress up so it sits around my hips. The window sash drops low enough that someone might be able to see. If not the details, then they might at least see the flashes of bare legs spread wide.

They would know that I'm standing spread-eagle, being ordered around, being used by a man. A wealthy man, one who can order three-hundred-dollars-a-glass whiskey for a woman he's only just met. A prostitute, basically. Someone he would pay for the hour.

I'll be imagining these in my sleep.

We'll never meet again after tonight.

There's shame in that.

And freedom.

He kneels behind me and fondles my ass. A quick slap of a hard hand on hot flesh, and I jump with a cry. It makes me push backward, where his mouth greets me with an impossibly intimate kiss. I gasp. He chuckles from the dark. "You're trying to drive me crazy."

"How? Me? No." I'm babbling, almost incoherent except that he understands me.

"Yes, you, beautiful. You're driving me crazy with this ass. This pussy. With that sound of shock like you've never had a man eat you out before."

"No," I moan as he works me with feathery licks at my entrance. Two fingers slide forward through my slick arousal to my clit, working it, working it, bringing friction and heat and a soul-shattering release. It pulls at my body in deep, wrenching rushes.

I thought of a million possibilities about tonight.

Of being hurt and being humiliated.

Of being afraid.

I never expected to climax.

A long shudder holds my body as luxurious pulses of my core seek something, not finding it. A tear leaks down my cheek. In the second of relief, I gasp a burning breath and slump against the cool windowpane.

"Delicious," he says, licking a line up the side of my throat.

He turns me to face the wall beside the window, the scroll pattern forming a texture against my bare breasts. His hand comes up between my breasts, wrapping around my neck. He tugs me back against him. His grip is only hard enough to make me gasp, not to withhold oxygen. It's a threat and a promise. It's a clench between my thighs.

"You'll let me do anything to you?" he murmurs.

"Yes," I moan, and he squeezes harder around

my throat in answer.

I never knew I had this side of me. Never knew it would make me shiver in arousal when a fist clenches in my hair, *hard*. He maneuvers me to the ground, not with word or gesture, but with the tension in my scalp.

First he angles me so that our lips almost touch. Made pliant by his dominance, my lips fall open. He kisses me hard, a marauder claiming territory as his own. My eyelids flutter and then fall, unable to bear the weight of his intense gaze.

Then he moves me to the base of his neck, to the hollow of his pulse. With my mouth only a centimeter away, with our kiss still a hot sensation on my lips, I know what he wants from me. I'm already licking, sucking at his rough skin before he mutters, "That's right. Kiss me. Lick me. Worship me."

The command makes me moan. I try to show him the same pleasure he shows me.

Then he moves me lower, lower, to the bulge in his slacks.

I can't properly lick or kiss him this way. Can't properly worship him through his slacks. In my current state of arousal that feels like a crime, so I graze my teeth against the fabric, gentle so I don't hurt him, but sharp enough that he feels the bite.

He grunts. "Dangerous little thing."

Then he drops me down, down, down.

My lips hover above the smooth shine of his dress shoes.

It's an act I've never imagined doing. It feels more filthy than some sexual acts, more intimate. And more delicious as I press a tender kiss to the curved leather.

"Good girl," he murmurs.

Then I'm on my hands and knees as he drags me across the plush carpet, my heels falling off behind me, completely naked in this opulence.

He drags me into the bedroom, but I barely have space to acknowledge the massive four-poster bed or the claw-foot tub I can see through the open bathroom door. I'm focused on the way he lifts me to standing, up on my very tiptoes. I'm so much shorter than him that he barely has to raise his arm to do so. I'm spinning under his casual manipulation, a clumsy, sensual ballet. Then he tosses me onto the bed, face-first. Plush bedding catches my fall.

I don't have time to recover before he covers me.

The blunt curve of something notches against my sex.

In my sensual daze, I recognize something: this might hurt.

Losing your virginity can hurt, right?

I don't know. Nothing feels real right now. Even time has spun out, turned liquid. He grips my hips, muttering something about not being able to wait, about ruining him, about needing to have me before he's gotten his fill.

He thrusts, and I freeze in a sudden, sharp stretch.

I'm not sure whether it's pain, but it's not pleasure.

It's a purgatory of feeling, a fierce clench to keep him out, a sigh of relief as he stays firmly lodged inside me. My thigh muscles tremble.

"Anne," he says, choking the name out.

There's a question in that word. *Why didn't you tell me?*

And primal satisfaction.

He must have felt it, too, the sense of something having torn, a barrier being broken. Irrevocable. Gone in a single thrust. He pulls back, and for a breathless, hollow moment I think he's going to be done with me. Then he pushes back inside with a harsh sound.

I'm too loose to hold myself up. My structural integrity has collapsed. I'm hugging the bed, palms flat, grasping at nothing, held up only by Will's hands on my hips and his cock in my pussy. He thrusts again and again, forcing me forward and back, using me with relentless drive, with dark command, turning my body into a toy for his own.

My second orgasm builds despite the faint burn.

Or maybe because of it.

My first climax was a tight knot. This is an endless spool of golden silk, spinning out for centuries, eternities, wrapping in on itself in an inexorable braid.

Only when the last of my innermost pulses have passed does he allow himself to let go, does he surrender to the pleasure, does he bite down on the place where my neck meets my shoulder with a feral growl. I brace myself through his peak, riding it out with slitted eyes seeing nothing and my hands clenched over his, holding him in the only way I can.

I would pool onto the crisp bedspread like liquid if he didn't pick me up.

It's like I weigh nothing in his arms like I'm petite and delicate as he pulls back the covers and lays me on the sheets. I'm like a princess. A pure princess laid in a tower.

The thought brings a smile to my drowsy lips.

A princess who's been despoiled.

Ravaged by the war that is higher education.

He disappears for a moment only to return with a warm washcloth. Suddenly shy, I put my hand between my legs to block him, a belated form of modesty. He waits, inexorable, infinitely patient, until I withdraw my hand. Only then does he clean me in the most private places, leaving me fresh and slightly cold beneath the air-conditioning.

He's gone again, and I hear water running.

A long pause.

It's only in the silence that real life begins to intrude.

I was swept away somehow, to an erotic dreamland where a thousand dollars and textbooks and societal condemnation didn't exist. It intrudes now with thoughts of him going downstairs to get cash from the concierge. Or paying me in Venmo.

Maybe he'll try to pay me with Bitcoin.

A slightly manic laugh threatens to bubble out of me.

When he appears again, he's wearing his suit slacks and nothing else, revealing a muscled chest with a tattoo design that curves across the side of his ridged abdomen. It looks like words written in an elegant, old-fashioned scroll. I can't see what it says, and my cheeks are already burning from checking him out.

The dress I was wearing disappeared, left behind in the aftermath of sex, probably pooled into a puddle of liquid near the window. My shoes are gone, too. I'm abundantly naked, still glistening from the washcloth.

The contrast between us, him clothed in suit pants and ink, me vulnerable, makes my stomach flutter.

His eyes aren't glinting with sexual desire anymore.

They aren't soft with satisfaction, either.

No, he looks pissed.

"Why didn't you tell me?" he demands.

Oh, that. "Tell you about what?"

"You know exactly what I'm talking about. Why didn't you tell me you were a virgin?"

"I probably should have. It does have six letters."

CHAPTER FIVE

Six Letters

I WAS NEVER a troublemaker. As a child, I learned that obeying adults and keeping my head down was the easiest path in life. Grown-ups barely knew I existed. My parents were busy with their lives. My teachers had a roomful of other children who threatened their standardized test averages. I flew under the radar, and that worked for me.

Except for Shakespeare.

Instead of enjoying English, I found it almost unbearable. Third graders read short vignettes about goldfish or recycling or the Mayflower. Multiple-choice questions tested our reading comprehension. *What is the main idea of this passage? Based on context clues, what does Joshua do before brushing his teeth?*

Who could learn to love reading under such a

barrage of boredom?

Ironically it wasn't until our science project that we took a class trip to the library, a small, cramped room in a large school. The books were frayed and yellowed, our reference material sorely outdated. I finished my work early, as usual, and wandered away while the teacher repeated herself and repeated herself.

It was pure vanity that drew me to Shakespeare.

I liked the way the books looked, tall and thick with leather binding and gold embossing. It was a contrast to the glossy colors and fingerprinted plastic covering on the other books.

I pulled out the thickest one, *Shakespearean Tragedies*, and started to read.

And kept reading even when the class was done, too engrossed in King Lear to notice. I stayed there through lunch and through afternoon gym class. I stayed until the librarian, an older woman with thick spectacles, turned off the light and locked the door behind her.

I spent the night there, curled up around thick volumes.

Maybe I was supposed to be scared?

All I knew was that it was blessedly quiet without my parents screaming.

No one noticed, of course. Not my third-grade teacher, Mrs. Slaughter, busy with her thirty other kids. Not the gym teacher, who never appreciated my dodgeball technique. Not even my parents, who probably thought having a daughter was a fever dream.

The person who seemed the most bothered by finding a bedraggled eight-year-old was the librarian. She'd taken me straight to the principal's office, a stern man who had proceeded to lecture me until my parents could be reached to pick me up.

It took hours.

He paced back and forth in his office, more frustrated than angry.

That's how Will looks right now.

He paces the bedroom floor, his weight leaving imprints on the heavy carpet behind him. Wearing down the fibers again and again. Unable to find the right words, even though he had so many just a few minutes before.

"Why the hell," he says again, struggling to keep his voice even, "didn't you tell me?"

I shrug, feeling the same buoyancy I did that morning.

I'm in trouble, yes, but I've also discovered an entirely new world. After that fateful night, the librarian slipped me my own key to the library. I could spend as long as I wanted in there as long as I got my schoolwork done. It became my haven.

This time the world isn't books. It's sexual desire.

Something unlocked inside me. And this man was the key.

"It doesn't matter," I say.

He growls. There's no other word for the sound. "It fucking matters."

He doesn't get to tell me what's important in my own body. Even if it does seem kind of important. Even if it feels like everything has changed. "Virginity is a social construct."

His eyes narrow. "Money is a social construct. Marriage is a social construct. Virginity is a very real thing that you had until about two minutes ago."

"Do you mean the protective membrane? Because I might not have even had it. I rode my bike a lot as a kid. And I've used tampons."

He pinches the space between his eyebrows. "Fuck."

"Listen, I didn't *want* to talk to you about tampons, but you brought it up."

"It's not the hymen," he says, biting off each word. "It's the fact that you've never done this before. I never would have taken you like that—rough and filthy and hard if I had known."

"I'm getting the feeling you wouldn't have done it at all if you'd known."

"Of course I wouldn't have."

I'm experiencing the same emotional roller coaster I had in that principal's office. At first I'd been drowsy and disoriented, almost bemused by the attention. Then I'd tried to bargain my way out of it. It had been a mistake. It wouldn't happen again.

When that failed, incipient anger started to grow inside me.

I had years of learning to tamp down that anger, to push it so far inside me it was invisible to everyone around me, a poison that leached through my blood and my blood alone. Only now it threatened to come out. Because what kind of strange irony was it that the one time I had to experience a lecture from the principal, it was for *reading*.

What kind of topsy-turvy upside-down world derided children for reading too much?

A world that valued rules and order over actual learning, that was for sure.

The secretary had popped her coiffed head into the room, her expression strained. "I'm trying to reach them," she'd told the principal. "No answer. I've called every number. Twice."

The principal frowned and sighed and glared at me as if this was my fault.

Which it was, in a way.

But it also wasn't.

"Do you see, Miss Hill?" he asked. "Do you see how you're inconveniencing everyone?"

The anger bubbled over.

I'd stood up, all forty-six inches of me and faced him down across a metal desk overflowing with detention slips and funding requests. "I don't see how *anyone* is being inconvenienced. I could be sitting in class right now playing the Oregon Trail after finishing my geometry worksheet, but instead I have to sit here listening to you tell me about right and wrong because you think I need to go home and change my clothes and eat a home-cooked meal and have my parents coddle me. But guess what? They aren't going to. It's Thursday, so my mom is at the hair and nail salon all day. My dad would never leave work to come get me. I'm pretty sure you don't even have the right phone numbers for them, because they don't want to hear from you. Or me. They're too busy with their own lives."

Whether it was due to pity over my lack of

parental support or whether he was impressed by my correct usage of the word *coddled*, the principal let me go to class.

I went home on the bus that afternoon like usual.

My parents never even mentioned the evening I was gone.

I suspected they never noticed. That they did notice and didn't care.

And now, in the present day, it happens again.

I'd landed in this bed dazed with sex endorphins. Then I'd tried explaining that it wasn't that big of a deal. If I wasn't worried about my virginity, why did it matter?

Then the anger bubbles over.

"My hymen or lack of it falls squarely under my business. The idea that any man, much less one that I've just met an hour ago deserves to make those decisions is just... That is just some... Some old-fashioned patriarchal bullshit."

I expect him to match my anger, to yell at me or storm out. Instead his stern expression softens, those dark eyes glint with something almost sweet. Is that appreciation? "You undervalue yourself. You could have sold your virginity for a hell of a lot more than a thousand dollars."

I raise my eyebrows. "How much more?"

"To someone who believes things about purity and innocence, someone who believes in... What did you call it? Some old-fashioned patriarchal bullshit? To someone like that it would have been priceless."

"You can always add it to the tip."

His lips quirk. "You assume that's me."

"I just watched you freak the fuck out about it."

"Because of the way I took you. I'd never have been so rough. So forceful. So...filthy."

I enjoyed that filth far too much. "In case you didn't notice, I climaxed."

"Twice, sweetheart. Don't think I didn't notice. How could I have missed it when you were clenching around my dick? Or spilling liquid arousal on my tongue?"

A shiver overtakes me. "So don't worry about how you did it."

Dark eyes glint with anticipation. "Oh, but I am worried."

"I'm perfectly fine."

"Fine isn't good enough." He stalks me, and I feel very much like prey. The bed is a wide-open clearing, absent of brush or tree trunks or anything to hide me. "Not for that sweet precious purity. Not for the innocent little lamb. You need more than fine."

Exhilaration runs through me. Along with desire.

Shocking to reach the age of twenty before knowing what true arousal feels like. The way I felt looking at a pop star or having a crush on a boy in class—none of them compare to this, as if there's lava running through my veins.

He takes off his belt. It makes a particular sound, leather through fabric loops. A sound that echoes in my bones. "Maybe I would have taken it easy on you," he murmurs, running two fingers along my thighs, making goose bumps rise. "A holdover from those old-fashioned times. But you don't need that, do you? You can take what I give you."

I'm highly aware of how naked I am, how bared I am to him.

The way my breasts rise and fall in exaggerated display. I understand flirting now. Not as a forced affectation. I understand it as the body's natural response. Fast breathing. Flushed skin. A sense of unlikely lightness. I don't know why I want to tease him, to prod him, but there's a sense of warmth that I can. We're strangers, the two of us, but we have this moment.

"Are you going to give me that belt?"

He takes both of my wrists and puts them above my head. "In a manner of speaking."

"This is how you'd treat a virgin?"

His eyes darken. "It's how I'd fantasize about it."

There's a sense of power there—being someone's fantasy. I turn my wrists, testing out the idea of confinement, trying it out with only the air to bind me. "You won't hurt me?"

"No," he says, then amends it. "Not really. Though I think you like it a little."

What a strange night. It's like I'm not really here. There's only the dream of me, a fantasy version of Anne Hill, someone who doesn't have to face him in the morning.

"Yes," I whisper.

He frowns. "What was that?"

"Yes, sir."

His arousal is obvious in his dress slacks, but it doesn't appear silly or even gauche. It's the way he's wholly unselfconscious about the bulge, the way he's focused far more on securing my wrists above my head. Wrapped leather feels snug against my skin, though it doesn't push into any particular place. As if it was made for me.

"Beautiful," he murmurs, trailing blunt-edged fingertips along the underside of my arm, over the hills of my breasts, through the slope of my stomach as I suck in a breath. "I want to hang you up on the wall. Put you on a white square pedestal in the museum."

"Like a statue? You give a new meaning to objectification."

He pushes two fingers inside me, a mute reproof. "A statue with power all through eternity. Admired by history. Made more beautiful by age. Desired and fought over and purchased by men. *Mad in pursuit and in possession so.*"

The words come automatically. "*A bliss in proof.*"

Slowly, slowly, he comes to a complete stop. A freeze. His hand hovers on my thigh. "Shakespeare," he murmurs. "You know it."

I've always had a good memory for words.

Not precisely a photographic memory, but if I read something, I can often recall it later. Sometimes I can even see it in my mind's eye: the style of font, where it was on the page.

Which is how I remember his sonnet on the perils of lust.

I never understood desire as a dangerous thing until tonight, the way it takes over my body, renders my reason mute. He describes lust in dark terms. "*Savage, extreme, rude, cruel.* That's what you meant by your games, isn't it?"

Expressions flash across Will's handsome face: surprise, interest, and finally, finally a kind of soul-deep bemusement. "Who the hell are you?"

"I told you," I whisper. "I'm nobody."

"Nobody." The angles of his face are hard as he drops his slacks and positions himself between his legs. "Nobody wouldn't make me so fucking hard I could turn to stone. Nobody wouldn't make me forget everything—my purpose here, my duty. Nobody wouldn't bring up Shakespeare while I'm hard as a fucking rock."

I pull and pull at the belt, not because I want to get free, but because I want to remain trapped. It's proof, you see. Proof that I'm safe. "Was he right? About the dangers of lust?"

"Here I am," he says, his thumb flicking my clit. "Fucking a virgin twice in a matter of minutes, heedless of her pain, her sensitivity, taking her because I can. Because I paid for the right. And because in this hellscape of a city, she's desperate enough to need it."

Then he's pressing inside me. I gasp at the invasion, at the sharp bite of pain, the reminder that I'm new to this. And I realize he was right. Virginity isn't only about a hymen or about inexperience. It's about the body accepting intrusion that has never come before. It's about invasion. Plundering. It's about surrender, and I surrender over and over again beneath him, arms above me, legs spread wide, looking up at his fierce expression.

He comes first with a roar, and it's that sound that pushes me over.

The release in aural form, the rumble in his chest. I'll never forget the sight of him in that moment, a vignette, a snapshot as my world narrowed and climax clenched down on my body. Through slitted eyes, I can only see a muscular shoulder and the dark of his hair framing a patch of white ceiling. Not his face or his cock. Nothing extraordinary at all, that curve, and yet it's the most intimate sight, something few people will ever see of him.

Then my eyes are closed, hot pinpricks pressing through tight lids. I force the tears back, because I haven't cried in years, and I'm not about to start now. I hold them back because he must sense that something is wrong anyway.

He curses and pulls away, abruptly ending our connection.

Gentle hands unwrap the belt from my wrists. This moment, breathing hard in the aftermath feels more exposing than him holding me up to the city, my breasts bared. More intimate than his cock inside me.

How embarrassing to feel as if I've lost something.

To feel uncertain after my virginity was taken, as if that means something in this modern age. Except somehow it does. It does, it does.

The worst part is that I don't regret it. I don't regret waiting, pushing away boys smelling of cheap beer and sweat, even though they got annoyed with me. I don't regret waiting for a stranger, *this* stranger, a man who knows what to do with my body.

He wraps me in his muscular arms and murmurs to me. *Brave girl. You're so sweet. I couldn't not take you. From the moment I saw you, I had to have you. You're mine.*

I realize that they aren't only meant to soothe me. They aren't sweet nothings.

They're his insides, exposed as surely as I was against the window.

His deepest secrets. His intimate soul.

Gifts made while his cum still warms my pussy, mingling with perhaps a hint of blood. I want the blood, I realize. I want it to symbolize something. Not pain, not loss. I want it to symbolize the fact that I've finally become a woman.

It's a doorframe.

I'm stepping through.

I walk and walk until I stand on a cliff, the whole of the night spread out in front of me. One more step and I fall straight down, into a dreamless dark, strong arms to hold me, to keep me safe, unaccountably—*Savage, extreme, rude, cruel*. All of those things, and also unexpected gentleness. A place to land as I sink into sleep.

CHAPTER SIX

French Toast

I WAKE UP alone.

The sensation comes to me first before the silkiness of the sheets, before the faint scent of lavender and lemon, even before the blessedly cool air-conditioning, which even with the windows streaming summer sunlight makes a cool cocoon around me.

I know I'm alone as surely as I can feel or smell anything else because it's so rare.

I'm never alone in the dorm rooms, where I share a two-hundred-square-foot space.

Daisy is a good roommate, but it's still tight quarters.

And past those thin four walls are hundreds of other kids.

Supposedly it's a random lottery system, but no one is surprised when the scholarship kids end up in Hathaway Dormitory, the one that's a single additional roof leak away from being condemned. Not everyone in the building is a scholarship kid. Sometimes other kids get unlucky. Our building is the equivalent of the short straw.

It's packed full, and that's how I know I'm alone now.

This is a suite that's probably as big as an entire floor of that building and it's empty, which means that sometime in the night Will left. He didn't wake me up and say goodbye. Why would he? He could have woken me up to kick me out, but he decided to let me sleep.

Why?

I don't know the etiquette. Not for a one-night stand.

And not for a paid one-night stand—or whatever this is.

Or maybe he didn't give me any thought. Maybe I meant as much as that large flat-screen TV and the gilded frame I can see through the bathroom door. Something he paid for.

Something he's done using.

I sit up in bed holding the lush blanket to my body with unnecessary modesty.

It's just that I don't belong here.

That sensation I felt ever since I walked into the lobby is back where even the walls are whispering: *get out, get out.* That sensation went away when Will approached me and stayed with me until now. Until he's gone. What does it mean that I felt belonging with him?

It's something I'd rather not think about, especially considering I'm never seeing him again. Which is a good thing. Because how horrifying would that be? I don't imagine our paths will cross. What grocery store or gym would we possibly go to that would be the same?

If I did run into him as part of some freak accident, it would be the worst.

A soft doorbell sound rings through the air.

Uh, the hotel suite has a doorbell?

Weird.

Who could be ringing it?

Will. That's my first thought. My heart jumps at the idea that he stepped out for some reason but came back...except there's no reason he would do that. No reason I'll ever see his handsome face again. Or hear his growly voice murmuring filthy words.

Besides the fact that he has a key card.

A fluffy white robe sits on the foot of the bed. I pull it on, trying not to marvel at the softness and the lemony scent. Then I pad across the heavy carpet to the door, where an older man in a white-collared shirt and black vest waits.

"Ma'am," he says, with all the gravity of a jury summons.

"Um. Yes. Hi."

He gestures behind him, where a cart covered in white cloth is laden with silver domes. There's also a coffee press and an assortment of small glass bottles of jams. "Your breakfast."

"I didn't get breakfast."

There's only the slightest pause. "I believe the gentleman may have ordered it."

The gentleman. My cheeks flame. Does he know what happened here last night?

Well, of course he knows we had sex. Embarrassment feels like actual fire on my skin right now. Lots of people have sex in hotels. It's nothing to be ashamed of, even if I'm not used to facing a random stranger about it in the bright of the day.

At least he doesn't know I was paid. Or maybe he does.

Maybe that was a little checkbox when he paid for the hotel room.

Will be using this hotel room for one hour only. Unless the girl falls asleep, in which case we'll let her stay until morning. That's how pathetic she looks.

Apparently I also looked hungry.

I stand back, throat tight, only able to gesture him inside.

Luckily he's very busy setting up rounded wings under the table cloth, pulling up one of the dining chairs, uncovering dishes with a steaming omelet, a stack of French toast, and a basket of thick, layered pastries.

It's only when he turns around, expression impassive, that I notice the en suite dining table from which he took the chair. There's my old model phone with its cracked screen and cheap case, the flower design faded to white where my hands hold it.

I put the phone there, along with the glittery black wristlet Daisy gave me.

I put the phone there last night, but I didn't put the stack of money underneath it.

That stack of money can only mean one thing.

It means the *gentleman* who sent my breakfast also paid for sex.

The server doesn't flush. He doesn't blink. I can't detect a single change in his grim expression. The sense of disapproval is only in the air. "May I get you anything else?"

The word *anything* could mean a basket of snakes the way he says it.

"No, thanks." The shame solidifies into a cold, hard wall around me. A protective shell. I may have slept with a man for money, but what right did it give him to judge me? What was so inherently noble about serving people pancakes that I, broke-ass college student and occasional woman of the night Anne Hill, was beneath him? "I trust the *gentleman* already tipped you."

He's already out of sight when the words spill from my lips, half caustic, half genuine.

There's a frigid silence. I don't turn and look at him.

"Yes, ma'am," he finally says.

When I'm alone again, I let out a long breath.

I pass by the gorgeous display of food with its fancy sliced fruit shaped like flowers and dots of what's probably honey emulsion or maple crema, heading for my phone.

The little light blinks telling me I have notifications.

Which is not a surprise. I always have notifications.

Always something broken that needs fixing.

Instead I push the phone aside and pick up the stack of money. I've never been particularly enamored of cold hard cash. It's always seemed like a taunt, how little I have, how quickly it slips through my fingers. The way there's never enough.

This is different.

It's a thick stack of hundred-dollar bills.

Even before I count them I know there's more than a thousand dollars.

There's *five* thousand dollars.

Holy shit.

Why did he give me so much more?

Because I spent the night?

Or because I didn't get home before midnight, after all? I do feel a bit like Cinderella, but only after her carriage turned into a pumpkin, the crushed detritus all around me. It's strange to hold money that represents what I did last night. It was embarrassing and probably degrading—but also transformative.

And it was, for the biggest surprise of the night, pleasurable.

Though I know, standing there naked underneath a fluffy robe, money in hand, that I can never, ever do this again. It wouldn't be the same with Saul or anyone like them.

It was…an anomaly. Beginner's luck, maybe.

It's only when I lift up the money that I see

the note underneath. The hotel's elegant letter-head is printed on the top. Masculine block letters sprawl across the small sheet.

Behind, a dream.

It's from the sonnet he quoted last night, the one about lust and the terrible, beautiful monster we become in those moments. And afterward, we're back to ourselves. The whirlwind of passion is a dream, one of both pleasure and shame.

Goose bumps rise over my skin.

I remember what he asked me, and I feel the same way in reverse. *Who the hell are you?*

Yes, a dream.

That makes far more sense than reality.

Then again, this stack of money feels real enough.

Finally I turn my attention to my phone. There's a bunch of missed calls from my mom. That's nothing new. Maybe it makes me callous that I don't rush to call her back, but I learned a long time ago how easy it was to be consumed by her life. There is always a new crisis. Always a new disaster, and I'm the one to fix it.

There are also texts from Daisy.

Where you at?

Talked to the bartender. He said you scored!

It's been like two hours, he's paying you extra, right??

I'm heading back to the dorm.

Listen, asshole, if you're reading this and you hurt my friend, know that I already flirted with the security guard to get the camera footage. You better leave the country unless you enjoy prison showers.

That last one makes me smile.

I dial her number.

She answers in three rings. "Tell me you don't need a hospital."

I glance down at myself in the robe, my dark hair in a wild mane over the fluffy white material. "I don't need a hospital."

"Thank God. The guilt would have been a bummer. I talked you into this."

"Flirting with the security guard?"

"Bluffing. But if you'd gone missing, I would have done it."

"I'm touched," I say, my voice dry. Even though I am. No one else would have cared, certainly. My parents might not even know. They would have just cursed me out for never coming to help them again, for not answering their calls.

What if a detective had come asking about me? They would have cried and bemoaned their own fates. Who would take care of them now? I know that without any bitterness. I love my parents in all their selfish, short-sighted glory. They are who they are.

We hang up with the promise for me to tell her everything when I get back.

I need to find my slinky black dress and make the walk of shame through the swanky lobby where bored, sleepy reception workers can judge me. I need to take this money home and hide it, possibly forever, this symbol of both my shame and my salvation.

But first, I needed to eat French toast.

CHAPTER SEVEN

Professor Stratford

I T IS A day caught between seasons where I'm hot in my sweatshirt, sweaty in the heat of the sun, where cold tendrils of fall reach beneath my clothes when I step into the long shadows of tall buildings.

Tanglewood University has a long and venerable history. It's a comforting mishmash of new buildings mixed with old technology and progress and the reminders of different times in rows of seating made for too-small bodies in double sets of bathrooms too close to each other. From a time when segregation was common, of buildings made without electricity.

Students clamor to get to class early in order to claim their places, some at the front of the class. Others around the edges staking a claim on the few plugs so they can charge their phones, their laptops, or in a few cases their Nintendo switches.

And then there are those in the back. The ones who want everyone else to know they're a little too cool for this. Me? I'm going to end up somewhere in the middle because as much as I would love to sit in the front row, I desperately need coffee if I'm going to make it through this day.

Plus, my wallet is thick with cash.

Of course, not thick with five thousand dollars.

Most of it safely stored beneath my dorm room mattress.

It's also dwindled down by a few hundred. I bought my economics textbook and some of my exam booklets that I'll need. I splurged on new pencils and those special white erasers that don't leave a mark. I was even tempted to buy this sweatshirt that was on sale for only five dollars if you were spending a certain amount showing off my pride in Tanglewood University.

I am proud of the school, but I am more proud of my presence here, of my ability to get in, not necessarily with grades because I've always been flush with those, but with the gumption it took to even send an application when I had no possible way of paying for it.

More proud of stumbling my way through my first year of college, not knowing if this would be my last. Taking each semester as a TV writer must take a season—giving it their all, knowing they might be axed before they get to the end.

There are three people in front of me at the coffee cart.

I glance at my phone. I won't be late, thank goodness, but it will be close.

"Hazelnut cream," a voice says behind me. "Two sugars."

I whirl to face Brandon, my ex-boyfriend. *Damn it.*

He's holding a steaming disposable cup with a picture of a coffee bean on it. "Hey, Annie," he says, his tone cajoling. "I know how you like it."

Of course, I don't want to accept his offering. We broke up. He knows that. He must have bought it a few minutes ago and been lying in wait. So why did he even buy it?

I glance back at the line. It's too long.

Reluctantly, I take the cup with a murmured, "Thanks."

Our fingers brush together, and I hide a flinch.

The first sip is a slice of heaven. I moan.

There's got to be something to be said about a guy who knows your coffee order, right? One who orders it in anticipation of seeing you?

Then again, sweet gestures were never Brandon's problem.

"What are you doing?"

"I wanted to see you." He looks so forlorn as he says it. "I've missed you all summer long. And then you stopped answering my text. My phone calls."

I give him my best severe look. "Because we broke up."

"Is that what happened?"

"Yes," I say, exasperated.

"Come on, Anne. Long distance was hard. I admit that. But we're both back on campus now. And you look great. Did I mention that?" When I roll my eyes, he continues. "No, seriously. There's something different about you."

Like the fact that I lost my virginity?

"We can pick up where we left off," he says.

That's not happening. "I heard that you had plenty of women to keep you company."

He rolls his eyes. "People like to gossip."

"Oh, so you didn't sleep with anyone?"

He pouts, and this is where I remember fully why we never worked. Why we never will. He's a twenty-year-old man-boy who pouts when he doesn't get his way. "You were so far away."

"Because you went to freaking Ibiza."

He looks around more concerned with whether anyone will hear me rather than the moral implications of his own actions. "I wanted to bring you with me."

Like a piece of luggage he could pay to have carted along. "I couldn't afford the tickets."

He rolls his eyes. "So stubborn."

I press the hot coffee to my forehead, letting it warm me. "Yes, stubborn enough not to text you back when I find out that you've been sleeping around."

"It didn't mean anything."

"The sad part is I believe you. It didn't mean anything to you, but it should. That's the problem." I hope it doesn't undermine my words that I take a sip and then another, because damn, this coffee is actually delicious and warm. I need it.

"I was just being wild. All the other guys have all this sex. I was just trying to keep up. Show them I was one of them. It was stupid, immature. You're not like that. You're better. You make me want to be better."

In a way, it's sweet because he's telling the

truth.

He does want me, or at least what I repre-sent—some version of a grown-up, caring relationship, but he doesn't know how to actually participate in one. He wants me to walk on his arm around campus and then he sleeps with random sorority girls at night.

"Look, Brandon, thank you for the coffee. I appreciate it, but I have to get to class."

He looks adorably crestfallen, adorable in the way that a small boy would look when being denied a treat. Then he brightens, looking determined, looking almost fierce. This is the face of the American golden child on campus, the one that everyone loves.

There's a building named after his grand-mother, for God's sake.

Of course, he was going to get admission to Tanglewood.

Of course he'd be able to pay for it.

And of course he could have bought my eco-nomics textbook for me just like he bought me this coffee. It would've meant nothing to him because it's not even his money.

But I earned it.

There are people who would think that there's shame in earning it the way I did, but I know that

I made this happen, this college degree. Every textbook, every class, everything.

"Goodbye, Brandon," I say, turning to climb the narrow stairs along with the last stragglers and make my way to room 346A. It is not as massive as the freshman weed-out classes. Not precisely a massive auditorium, but neither is it small.

About a hundred seats have held students for a hundred years and little desks make it hard to write. I shove my bag beneath the seat and take out a notebook.

"Do you know who's teaching this?" the guy next to me asks. He has sandy hair. I've seen him around in our classes. We're probably on the same major track.

I can't quite remember his name. Tyler. Travis.

I shrug. "I thought it was Oglevy."

Professor Oglevy is a dinosaur. She's been at Tanglewood University since forever. Basically, not only teaching as a tenured professor but also doing her undergrad as one of the first women ever admitted into this university.

For the most part, I like her.

She's smart, thoughtful, informative, if a little scatterbrained. Though when I had her for Intro to Literature, she tended to mark me down for reasons I still don't fully understand.

I'm used to getting straight As even from the tough professors.

I'm used to them leaving marks scrawled on my papers in Sharpie with comments like *great insights* or just an enthusiastic *yes* underlined three times.

Whereas Professor Oglevy leaves longer notes written in her signature purple pen. *Dive a little deeper*, she says. *Reach beneath the surface. There's something there for you, Ms. Hill. It's written between the lines.*

Except I examined *The Merchant of Venice* to within an inch of its life. I knew every bit of symbolism, every metaphor, every historical context. What was I missing?

However, I was perfectly fine taking this course with her. I was fine taking my cryptic comments and reluctant As. It didn't affect my GPA. Didn't risk my scholarship.

Tyler or Travis or whoever he is, shakes his head. "She's gone."

"What?"

"Leave of absence."

"What happened?"

He smirks. "Heard she got caught on Only-Fans."

SKYE WARREN

My face makes an involuntary expression. I am as sex positive, age positive, and overall not positive as the next girl, but I really don't think that frizzy gray-haired Mrs. Oglevy was on that app. "Maybe she had a death in the family."

He shrugs. "Who cares? Either way, she is not teaching anything this year. This semester they got Davis to teach Intro to Lit."

Maybe he would be the one to teach this class to teach Shakespeare's tragedies. Though he already has his own classes and his own research, which he's quick to point out to any student at any time, is far more important than their most rudimentary understanding of important texts. So I can't imagine him taking on a professor's full load.

Now that I notice it, there's an air of expectation in the classroom. Do they all know that we're expecting someone new or is it something else? Something more ethereal. A sense that things will be different this semester.

I take a fortifying sip of coffee. *Thank you, Brandon.*

Maybe they'll bring someone in. I haven't seen it too much. In our specific department, there is a lot of posturing, a lot of talking shit about other literature departments and how no

78

one can measure up and how exclusive they're with hiring. But I've seen it happen in other classes. My sociology class was taught by someone from Princeton who was standing in when our regular teacher was on maternity leave.

Tyler snorts. "Good luck to whoever the hell it is. At least we don't have to hear about Oglevy's cat anymore."

Twinkles made it into a surprising number of stories about medieval literature. But no matter how exasperating I found that, I wasn't about to agree with Tyler out loud. The sad truth is that academia is still a man's world, and even though women contribute to research just as much, if not more, they are still given less credit and more criticism.

The lecture hall has two entrances. One near the front of the room where all of us entered. It's usually where the professors enter, too, bustling in with laptop bags or old-school briefcases, cheeks pink from the short walk from the Center for Humanities Research, the newer, shinier building. The offices were smaller, but they had far more reliable central air.

The lecture halls in this building had offices attached from a time when professors taught in the same room. Those rooms are often empty, ghost rooms, used as temporary workspaces by teaching assistants who weren't high enough in the pecking order to warrant a regular cubby in CHR. It should be empty, the office attached to this lecture hall, but the door swings open.

Tyler is still talking—something about us trading phone numbers so we can swap notes in the class. I can barely hear him, because I'm so focused on what's happening in front of me. The dark eyes. The strong jaw. The body beneath a tweed fucking coat. Tweed. It should be illegal for a man to look hot in tweed, but somehow he managed it.

I wish he was a stranger.

I wish to God I didn't know what it felt like to have him over me, under me, surrounding me. To have him be the air I breathe, the sounds I make.

It's him.

Will or whatever the hell his real name is.

My first and only customer.

The man from the hotel.

Horror zings down my spine. Shock holds me frozen.

No, this has to be a dream. I'm going to wake up and be back inside my dorm room.

Or maybe I'm still sleeping in the fancy hotel

suite, breathing in the surprisingly pleasant musk of him. In this version I don't wake up alone. In this version when I open my eyes, he's beside me, tangled around my body, handsome face relaxed in sleep.

Except it's not a dream.

"Professor William Stratford." He's not even facing us, but his voice booms through the lecture hall. "This is Advanced Comparative Analysis of Literature. If you're not in the right class, leave. If you are in the right class, let's get to work."

He turns to face us, his expression stern. No one moves.

People are wide-eyed. There are whispers in the crowd.

Everyone is seeing him. And some of them seem to know him?

Yes, well. I know him.

I know him as my not-quite sheep farmer on emerald hills in Ireland.

As my rare books dealer.

Despite my shock, or maybe because of it, I'm tempted to laugh out loud.

You're a rare book dealer. The successful kind.

That was my guess based on fantasy, based on flirting.

You could say that, he answered.

Yes, you could, considering he teaches. He's my new professor.

CHAPTER EIGHT

Enter Sampson and Gregory

H E DOESN'T GLANCE at the rows of students—at me. Instead, he walks to the chalkboard and writes in large block letters: ROMEO AND JULIET. Panic beats in my breast.

The hard strokes of chalk bring the room to a ringing silence.

"You've all read the play," he says, his confident voice filling the hollow space. "Or I don't know how the hell you made it this far. You've watched the movies. Seen *West Side Story*. Maybe read the anime. So what's it about?"

There's a moment of stunned silence.

I'm busy panicking about my own personal tragedy, but distantly I recognize the general confusion of everyone else. This isn't how classes go, especially not the first classes.

First classes are for the professors to introduce themselves, to put the syllabus on the projector and talk about the breakdown of our grades. If we do start actual work, it's general. Professor Oglevy had a particular story about her cat catching a bird as a metaphor for "Beowulf" that she liked to tell. Even if we were going to discuss an entire play, we'd need notice. There should have been a prerequisite reading list with discussion questions.

"A tragedy," someone throws out.

That earns him a nod. "Meaning what?"

"Meaning they die," someone else says.

There's a sprinkle of nervous laughter.

"That's it? That's the point? Seems like we don't need three hours for people to die."

"It's a love story." A feminine voice this time.

He turns around, and that's when it happens. That's when he sees me. Our eyes lock. Recognition. Shock. Awareness. I watch all of it pass through his eyes, even though the rest of his expression remains impassive. Can anyone else read him?

No, I don't think so. They're still talking about a play written in 1595.

A love story, of all things. A tragedy.

Someone scoffs. "They're teenagers."

"How old are they?" he asks, his voice a shade

lower. Closer to what it was in bed.

"Thirteen," someone says.

Juliet is thirteen years old. Young. Too young to get married, even in that time. And her father initially thinks so, too. But somewhere along the way, crucially, he changes his mind. He changes the course of her life. He sets his child on a path toward death.

Professor Stratford meets my eyes, and in that dark gaze I see the night we spent together in vivid detail—both the sensuality and the tragedy of it. "What about Romeo?" he asks, not breaking eye contact. "How old is he?"

If this were any other class, if he were any other professor, I might open my mouth. I might contribute, but not now. I can't imagine speaking. My voice would probably come out as a squeak. Or worse, a sexual whimper.

How old is Professor Stratford? Definitely an adult.

That was abundantly clear in the hotel bar, but it's even more pronounced as he stands in a roomful of barely grown, gangly, mostly teenaged boys. They're wearing torn T-shirts and backwards ball caps while he has on brown slacks and a white dress shirt. He doesn't wear them stiffly. They're neat, tucked in, and yet seem perfectly comfortable on his strong body.

His square jaw is perfectly smooth now, but I remember the feel of his scruff against my skin, the delicate scratch. I shiver beneath his regard now, somehow wanting it again. The desire mixes with my existential horror, because my worlds have collided.

"Fourteen," comes the murmured answer behind me.

"Fifteen," Tyler corrects, sounding confident.

I can't stay for this.

I'll talk to the registrar, even though I already know I need this class. I grab my messenger bag and prepare to sneak out, for all the world as if I have to go to the bathroom or take a phone call. People leave all the time without comment, but Professor Stratford's gaze finds my messenger bag, and then me. I freeze.

"Are you sure?" Professor Stratford asks him, an almost mocking tilt to his head.

Tyler shifts in his seat. "We read this in ninth grade. It's childish."

"Ah, yes," he says, though the softness in his voice doesn't sound like agreement. "Perhaps you'd rather discuss *Hamlet*. Would that be more mature?"

"Sure," he says, clearly uncomfortable. "At

least it's about a prince."

I tense, prepared for a hard set down. I'm not Tyler's greatest fan, but I still don't particularly want to see him humiliated in front of the entire classroom. And somehow I know that this man, Professor Stratford, or Will, the man from my most shameful night, could do it. He wants to. It's held inside his intractable body.

No, no, no. Do not call on me, Professor Stratford.

"What do you think, Ms...."

I clear my throat. "Ms. Hill."

"Do you think *Romeo and Juliet* is childish?"

It's even worse. He doesn't want to humiliate Tyler. He wants me to do it. "No."

"Explain."

I'm aware of Tyler beside me, as well as the man standing in front of me two rows down. It might as well be the three of us in the large auditorium. Then Professor Stratford's lip quirks up in what I take as encouragement, and Tyler fades away. It's only the two of us here. We might be on a bed as soft as a cloud, high above the city in a suite. We might be naked. That's how intimate the moment feels. That's the only reason the truth comes out of me.

I open my clenched fist and let the messenger

bag slide to the floor. "Romeo isn't fourteen. Or fifteen. Or a teenager at all. It's something that even serious analysis texts and encyclopedias get wrong. The truth is that the play never gives him an age, so it's up to the reader to decide."

He stares at me. Expressions flash across his face in rapid succession: surprise, interest, and a kind of soul-deep bemusement. So similar to that night. *Who the hell are you?* he asked.

I'm nobody.

I didn't want him to call on me, but now that he has, I'm going to answer honestly. "People say he's a teenager because he acts young. Falling in love quickly. Being moody. But don't older men do that, too? It doesn't prove he's a teenager."

He nods slowly. "Perhaps society is so intent on him being a teenager because it makes them uncomfortable, the idea of an older man with a younger woman."

Nobody, he said that night. *Nobody wouldn't make me so fucking hard I could turn to stone. Nobody wouldn't make me forget everything—my purpose here, my duty. Nobody wouldn't bring up Shakespeare while I'm hard as a fucking rock.*

"But the other reason that *Romeo and Juliet* isn't childish, the main reason, is that it's about a young woman taking charge of her life in a society determined to strip her of her agency. What is more grown up, more mature, than taking control of your life?"

His dark eyes contain an entire universe. "Very good," he murmurs.

My sex clenches as if he's praising me for a sexual act.

Someone raises their hand in the front row, and after a long moment, Professor Stratford nods at them to speak. "But is it really good to take control of your life if it ends that badly?"

"A good question," he says, finally turning away from me. "What do you all think? Would you rather have a safe life that you don't control? Or a dangerous one that you do?"

It gives the class pause.

Then there's a burst of discussion.

"I'd rather control my own destiny, even if it doesn't work out."

"Not for me," says a guy who looks like a jock. "Give me a nice house, a cook, and cleaning staff, I'll marry whoever you want."

The class laughs.

Someone near the back speaks up. "Can we really say that a life married to Paris would have been safe? Women didn't have rights. If he would have been cruel or even abusive, she would have had no choice but to stay."

That sobers everyone.

Professor Stratford looks satisfied. "This is Advanced Comparative Analysis of Literature, ladies, gentlemen, and others. Agency. Control. Danger. Identity." He pauses, and I feel the way he does *not* look at me so acutely it's like passing beneath one of the large buildings—cold and dark. Shocking after the warmth of his regard. "Sex."

There's a titter of laughter at the word.

There's a podium for him to stand at with a microphone, but he clearly doesn't need it. Nor does he sit down at the large table with a desk chair behind it. Instead he sits on the table, his legs hanging down, supremely comfortable in front of a hundred curious eyes.

He produces a small book from his back pocket, worn and yellowed from years of use. I don't recognize the cover, at least not from this far away. It's not from the library. His personal copy, then. He opens it to the beginning. "Enter Sampson and Gregory, with swords and bucklers, of the house of Capulet."

He points to Tyler. "Sampson." A girl named Dara gets assigned the role of Gregory, one of the two servants arguing in the opening scene. "Come to the front of the room. Shakespeare is meant to be heard aloud, so we're going to speak it."

There's some grumbling as the two get up and climb down.

They're nervous as they stumble over the old-fashioned words.

Professor Stratford has a surprising amount of patience for pronunciation, not bothering to correct them when it's blatantly wrong, murmuring helpful prompts when they get stuck.

He only stops us every few verses to discuss what was read, both the literal interpretations and the symbolic ones. And unlike other professorial discussions I've seen, he actually wants us to voice our opinions on what's happening.

I'm used to teachers grading us based on how closely our words mimic whatever the lauded experts think. In contrast he presents those as only one possible option, allowing us to bring our own ideas and perspectives to the text.

I learn more about myself from this process.

And I learn more about my classmates, like the fact that Sunita's parents had an arranged marriage. Like the fact that Anthony's father was shot by a rival gang in the street when he was a child. Like the much more fact that the two warring fraternities of Tanglewood University have a feud stretching far back that even friendship between its members is forbidden.

"What if two of its members fell in love?" Professor Stratford asks.

There's quiet, because for all that the world has changed, we know there are still dangers.

Prejudice in the most traditional sense, two men falling in love.

The feud would only make it worse. Would it end in violence? Maybe. Probably. Which shows that we aren't nearly as evolved as we like to think we are.

Professor Stratford calls from the classroom to read each scene, even changing the person playing a single character so that more have a chance. Earlier in the class, Tyler and Dara stumbled over their words, clearly uncomfortable with being singled out.

Toward the end the ones chosen almost seem excited to hurry down. They provide more dramatic exclamations and gestures as they get more involved in the play.

The reader of Capulet, a boy with shaggy hair and skinny jeans, gives special weight to the words, *My child is yet a stranger in the world.* She's too young for marriage. That's what he says, and he's right, he's right. So why does he change his mind later? Why does he then betroth her to Paris? The weight of that worry hovers in the air, transforming an ordinary, dusty auditorium into a shared experience.

This is more than analysis.

More than understanding.

It's embodying. It's living inside the pages, seeing them from the inside out.

The discussion invigorates me, despite my persistent anxiety.

What if he's going to fail me because of what happened?

He called on me with a question, but what if I said the wrong thing?

I sink a half-centimeter lower in my seat.

"That's the end of scene three," Professor Stratford says as the last readers climb back into their seats. "That's why it takes three hours for people to die. You feel it, don't you? The weight of your worry, the knowledge of the tragedy to come? Foresight isn't always a gift. It's certainly not a gift from William Shakespeare in this play."

The old-style bell rings through the halls, marking the end of ninety minutes. The newer buildings don't have bells. Only this old one has it, its slightly tinny sound ringing through vaulted ceilings. Usually when it sounds everyone grabs their stuff and rushes the door, even if the professor is still speaking. This time they only watch.

Professor Stratford nods. "Let me know if you have questions. Or don't, because I'll explain the assignments when we get there. Next class, our Romeo will meet his Juliet."

Only then does everyone rise in a bustle of backpacks, laptops, and jackets.

He stands and finally, finally looks at me. "Ms. Hill. See me in my office."

My cheeks turn warm, and probably pink, but he doesn't see since he turns and leaves the classroom through the private door.

"Damn," Tyler says. "First class and you're already in trouble?"

Apparently.

I grab my messenger bag and sweater and follow him, keeping my head down so I don't meet anyone's eyes. Am I in trouble because of what I said, my analysis of Romeo's age and Juliet's agency? Or am I getting called into his office to discuss that night in the hotel?

Either way I'm not looking forward to the conversation that comes next.

Whatever happens, he won't be pleased.

And I learned long ago how little power I have

over my own life.

I'll have to hold on with both hands. What happened that night can't affect this class. It can't affect my college career or my future. I won't let it.

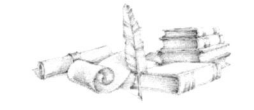

CHAPTER NINE

A Little Leverage

T HE FIRST THING that strikes me is the rich scent of old books mingling with the faint aroma of aged wood. The room is dimly lit, with sunlight filtering through heavy curtains, casting a warm, amber glow over the space. The walls are lined from floor to ceiling with towering bookshelves, crammed with dusty tomes of various shapes and sizes, some bearing faded leather bindings and others with yellowed pages.

In the center of the room sits a large, mahogany desk, its surface cluttered with papers, journals, and a spill of pens. It's a place where ideas are born, where knowledge is revered, and scholarly traditions are honored.

It's also the place where I face the man who took my virginity.

Professor Will Stratford stands behind the

desk, looking imposing. His expression is more severe than it was in the bar, almost angry. Maybe this is what surprise looks like on him.

God knows *I'm* shocked. Horrified. Appalled.

How could this have happened?

We drove so far out of Tanglewood proper so we wouldn't be recognized.

"What were you doing in Cressida City?" I blurt out, not that it really matters. I suppose rich people go out for drinks at expensive hotels. Or maybe he went there to find a woman like me, one he could pay for the night. One he could make crawl on the floor.

It doesn't matter why he was there, but it's the only thing I can think of to ask.

I'm not sure whether I really expect him to answer.

I definitely don't expect him to laugh.

It's a harsh, bitter sound.

"How much?" he asks.

I flash back to that night. How much for the night? Presumably he doesn't mean that we're going to have sex again. In this old-fashioned office. No. "What?"

"How much to keep this quiet?"

I blink. "Excuse me?"

"Don't play stupid, Ms. Hill. It doesn't suit

you."

Frustration bubbles inside me, along with an inconvenient sense of pride. He thinks I'm smart. "I have just as much of an interest in keeping this whole thing quiet as you do."

He gives me a dire expression that unfortunately goes straight to my pussy. "This is my career we're talking about."

"This is *my* college degree we're talking about, too."

"It wouldn't be you they would blame, sweetheart." The endearment sounds caustic, nothing like the melodic praise he gave me that night. "You weren't the authority figure in this situation. You're practically a child."

My eyes narrow. "I'm twenty years old. An adult."

"And my student."

"You didn't know that at the time."

"They won't care. Are you honestly trying to tell me that you didn't plan this?"

"Why on earth would I have planned this?"

"You spend one night playing a confused little ingenue for your professor. And in return you get…blackmail money. A guaranteed A in the class."

Shock renders me speechless for long seconds.

"Fuck you."

"You can't expect me to believe this wasn't planned."

"I don't need to sleep with a teacher to get an A."

Heat pricks my eyes, but I refuse to let tears fall. I refuse to let him see them. I haven't cried in years, not over filth or abuse or even losing my virginity.

I'm sure as hell not going to start now.

Confused little ingenue?

Fuck him.

Well, I suppose I already did that.

I turn blindly to leave before I can fall apart. He moves faster than he should be able to, his large palm landing on the door to block my exit. I stare at the back of his hand, the faint dusting of hair. And beneath, light freckles. Those make him look almost human.

Luckily I've seen to the heart of him, so I know he's not.

"Let me leave."

"So you can run to the dean's office."

"How dare you." I force composure onto my face before I whirl to face him. "If I *did* go to the dean's office and tell him what happened that night, it would only be the truth, wouldn't it? But

I'm not going to do that. You know why?"

He doesn't answer, instead watching me with that same casual mastery he used in class, the one that tempted and taunted us to actually share what we thought.

"Because they always blame the woman. Oh, maybe they would fire you or demote you or whatever the hell they can do to rich-as-hell professors who like whiskey, but they will whisper about the harlot who tempted you down that path. My name will become legendary in this field, not for what I know but for who I had sex with."

He studies me, his eyes narrowed. "If people did find out," he says, more slowly than before, "it would only be the truth. So why risk it if you're so afraid of that?"

Those tears threaten again. "Because it was the only way to get the money I needed for my economics textbook. And the exam booklets we need, because even though my scholarship is a full ride, it doesn't cover those. How do they *think* we're going to pay for them?"

"Anne—"

"No, you don't get to call me that. I'm Ms. Hill. And you're Professor Stratford."

His expression goes blank, and I almost wish I

could take the words back. I'd rather have his anger, even his derision, over the cool implacability of the professor. "Ms. Hill. Why not go farther away?"

I scoff. "Do you think I have a car? No, I rely on the Tanglewood Metro system. Or I spend money I don't have on an Uber, using the cheapest option possible, sharing the ride with someone who might try to grope me in the bathroom."

He looks slightly bemused, as if poverty hasn't occurred to him. "You make one thousand dollars an hour."

I can't help but roll my eyes. "I made ten dollars an hour at the library as part of my work-study program. That night was the first and *only* time I ever did that."

Skepticism darkens his handsome face. "Really?"

It's not a question. More of an accusation. "Yes, really."

"What about your friend?"

My friend has done it many more times. "That's none of your business."

"It is if she's in on the blackmail. The night I'm back in Tanglewood. The night I get roped into attending that godforsaken black-tie event.

The only night I gave in to—"

"Gave in to what?"

He shakes his head, his dark gaze never leaving mine. "You looked new."

"I looked…new?"

"Green. Nervous. Young as a lost little lamb."

"So you're insulting me now."

"That's why everyone in that bar was staring at you, men and women alike. The room was full of predators. You felt it. That's what made you scared. They wanted to devour you."

Despite the gravity of the situation, despite the fact that he's only a few inches away from me, despite the fact that I can scent his masculine musk, that I remember it, that it makes my body clench, I laugh. "No one noticed me."

"They were preparing to pounce, especially with your friend gone."

"If anyone pounced, it was you."

"That's right," he says, his tone almost speculative. "I took what I wanted for the first time in…years. Decades. Too damn long." A rough laugh. "The last time it nearly cost me everything. And this time? I'm still waiting to hear what it will cost."

My eyes narrow. "There's no blackmail. There's no setup. There's no anything except a girl who was desperate enough to go into a locked room with a stranger. You made me come. You took my virginity, and what's worse? You liked it."

I fling the words like arrows, hoping to wound him.

Hoping to make him retreat.

He doesn't.

Instead he steps closer, pressing me against his desk. How did I get here? Suddenly carved wood presses into the back of my thighs, cool even through my worn jeans. He's standing over me, forcing me to lean back.

Predator. The word comes to mind along with its opposite.

Prey.

"I didn't like it," he murmurs, the words like warm velvet over my skin, an illicit caress. "I fucking loved it. You did, too. I never wanted to pay for sex. It wouldn't be real, anyway. She wouldn't really want it. Then I saw you, so beautiful and tragic. So fucking vulnerable."

Tragic? "How dare you?"

"Oh, I dared to bring you upstairs, to put my fingers in your wet little hole, to fuck you until you cried. I dared to live out every fantasy with you that night, secure in the knowledge that I would never see you again."

"I wish," I say, but I'm feeling a little breathless. A little warm.

"Do you want to know the worst part? I missed you. Having you, knowing how good you felt around my cock, squeezing and panting and writhing like a little minx, it only made me hotter for you. I burned up the bedsheets the next night and the next, my cock hard and nowhere to go."

"Go back to the hotel," I manage, even though the idea of him selecting someone else from the bar makes bile rise in my throat. "Find another girl."

"I don't want another one. I want you."

The words should not make my heart beat faster. They should not make me flush with pride. It's too bad my body doesn't know that. "You had your fun. It's over."

"You moaned for me. Came for me. I can make it happen again."

"You can't," I gasp, though I don't know whether it's shock or arousal moving me. Maybe both. Maybe they're like some unholy partnership.

He proves me wrong, of course. He proves me wrong by brushing his lips across my forehead. Such a simple action. Almost chaste. At least, it should be. But it makes a mockery of chasteness, that warmth. It sends an electric spark down my spine. It makes my thighs clench together...and a small breathy moan escapes me.

His lip curls into a knowing smile. "There's my girl."

"I'm not...yours." The words come out slurred, especially when he puts his large hand on the inside of my thigh, when he pushes my legs apart and steps between them. It cants my body upward, and my elbows fall back to hold my weight. In this position I can't guard myself from him. He looks down at my body with pure hunger.

"Do you know how hard it was for me to stand in front of a class of a hundred people, wanting you, hard for you? The tip of my cock slick with pre-cum for you?"

Somewhere deep inside I find the courage to ask. "How hard?"

He nudges me between my legs, making me feel his throbbing erection, hot and impossibly thick. "If it was just your body, just your gorgeous lips, I might have survived it. Then you had to go and speak. You had to say something no one has said in an undergraduate class. Something that was fresh and interesting and so fucking smart I could have climaxed."

That makes me want to tease him. "You have a smart kink?"

"Hell yes. And it's a real problem."

He says it in a growly tone that is sweet compared to his derision before. I want more of this, except he's right. This *is* a problem. I need this class. I'm going to have to sit in that lecture hall every week for the entire semester.

If he was worried about blackmail, then it means he doesn't want anyone to know, either.

So the secret is safe.

We're safe.

As long as we don't kiss again.

As long as he doesn't look at me like he wants to devour me.

Too late.

I need to push him away somehow. As the professor he has all the power in this situation, but I need something of my own. A little leverage. A little...knowledge. And I do have that, don't I? He's given me tiny windows into his world.

I'm angry at myself. For letting myself be dragged back to this godforsaken city, where I have to pretend like everything is fine, like I'm not walking through a battlefield.

I look into his dark eyes, breathe his air. I

want him, but I can't have him. Not ever again. "Why do you hate Tanglewood so much?"

The question works. As a weapon. As a defense. His eyes shutter. The desire? Gone. Or at least masked by that hard professor exterior. "Why do you like it?"

My mom and dad always spoke of Tanglewood with fearful tones, as if the sin and the vice of the city might reach all the way into the rural farmhouses. The truth is, the city didn't care about us. It's lit up while we lived in the dark ages.

I wanted to go to Tanglewood University since I knew it existed.

It's been my dream. I won't let anything stop me.

Not an overpriced economics textbook.

Not my inconvenient desire for this man. "It represents freedom."

He nods. "That's what the rest of the world represents to me."

"Then why are you here?"

"To risk my entire career on a single night with a woman young enough to be my daughter, apparently."

His dry answer tickles unlikely humor inside me. It shouldn't be funny. We're both at risk, but something about being in this office alone with him, with our shared confidences decorating the air, makes me feel…intimate. Even more intimate than when he was inside me that night in the hotel. "I'm not going to tell anyone."

"I'm not going to tell anyone either."

Relief fills me. Disaster averted. If neither of us tells, then neither of us can get in trouble. Thank God he's no longer looking at me with that cold suspicion. Though he doesn't seem precisely comforted, either. He seems tense. "Then…that's good, right?"

"Good?" That earns me a caustic laugh. "I wouldn't use that word. Painful. Ironic. Maybe even tragic, considering how badly I want to fuck you on this desk."

CHAPTER TEN

Extra Credit

*P*AINFUL. IRONIC. MAYBE *even tragic, consider-ing how badly I want to fuck you on this desk.* My body tightens as if preparing for him. "You...do?"

"I shouldn't, of course."

"Of course not," I murmur, breathing in the scent of his musk. His arousal.

"We both know how that would end."

With both of us disgraced. "Foresight isn't always a gift."

"No, it's not," he mutters, running blunt fingers up the side of my arm.

I shiver. We might as well be in a suite at the hotel in the moonlight, that's how my body responds. It warms, tightens. It turns incredibly sensitive, attuned to the slightest touch. My body doesn't seem to know that we're in the middle of a dignified office with sunlight landing on dust motes. It feels like a betrayal, that latent arousal. Like I'm not even myself anymore.

I push off the desk, forcing him to step back.

I immediately miss the heat of him, the feeling of being pinned down.

Why did he release me? It's a ridiculous question, because the alternative would be cruel. The aroused part of me wants him to hold me down. It wants him to force me, so I wouldn't have to argue with myself anymore. So I could have him.

A good student would leave the office.

She would pretend this never happened, pretend she doesn't know how good his body feels. Unfortunately, I'm not a very good student. Instead I wander over to the bookshelf, unable or unwilling to walk out the door.

There's a film of dust on the old tomes, obscuring the faint gold embossing on the leather spines. "Are you going to clear these out?"

"No." His voice is terse.

I glance back, curious despite myself. "Why not?"

"Because with any luck, I won't be here next year."

My eyes widen. "Where would you go?"

"Anywhere. But most likely back to DC."

"Washington, DC? Are you in politics?"

He gives me an enigmatic smile, a clue that there's some deeper answer I'm not nearly deep enough to know about. "Absolutely not. I mostly worked on my books. And consulted for the Folger Library. Gave talks, that sort of thing."

Holy shit. The Folger Shakespeare Library is incredibly prestigious. They have some of Shakespeare's original manuscripts, as well as artifacts like playbills and stage costumes.

I can't believe someone with that cache is teaching a bunch of sophomore idiots like us. That's the beauty of being at a world-class university like Tanglewood. It's why I'm so lucky to have my scholarship.

Something he said makes me pause. "Your books?"

One large shoulder lifts in a shrug. "I am a rare book dealer, actually. Or a rare book author. I write obscure analysis texts that scholars put on their shelves to gather dust."

"About *Romeo and Juliet*?"

His smile is self-deprecating. "That would be far too broad for a truly pedantic scholar. I can write paragraphs upon paragraphs about the potential meanings of a single stage direction."

"Exit, pursued by a bear," I say, repeating one

of his most infamous stage directions from *A Winter's Tale*, one both humorous and difficult to produce on stage.

His lips quirk in acknowledgment. "I can write entire chapters about the portrayals of cross-dressing. An entire book dissecting the depictions of courtship rituals."

"Such as appearing beneath your lover's window?"

"Such as asking for your phone number under the guise of wanting a study partner."

My cheeks heat, remembering Tyler's last question before class started. Professor Stratford heard that? "What do you think?" I ask, working hard to keep my voice light. "Of his request? Should I give him my number?"

"Subterfuge is the provenance of the young."

"Spoken like a truly pedantic scholar," I say, faintly mocking.

He inclines his head, ceding the point. "I prefer the direct approach."

"Like asking someone to have sex for one thousand dollars."

His eyes burn with sensual memory. "Even seeing you in the classroom today can't make me regret what happened. It was the most erotic night of my life."

Surprise and pleasure rush through me. It was? This is not some young frat boy who gets excited by a kiss in the back seat. This is a man with real experience. And this was the most erotic night? "Is that why you left five thousand instead?"

"I left five thousand because I'm not in the habit of taking advantage of young women who clearly need the money, who would have dutifully lay under me regardless of whether I'd made you come." His eyes darken. "Even though you *did* come. I'm haunted by the feel of you clenching around me."

A shiver overtakes me. "And should I give Tyler my number?"

He prowls close to me, and I realize that somewhere in our conversation I wandered back to the center of the office—in the perfect position for him to back up against the desk once more. Did I do it on purpose? Do I want him so badly that my subconscious is offering me up?

This close I can see the faint blue striations in his eyes. His eyes aren't black, though they look that way from a distance. This close he's the expanse of ocean in the dark night. "Do you think Tyler could make you come until you moan, until your whole body shakes?"

"Maybe," I whisper, even though—no, no, of course not. No one can. Except him.

He lets out a sound that can only be described as a growl. "Perhaps I should give you another one, a reminder of what it feels like, so you can compare when he fumbles around."

I whimper, unable to say no, unable to beg for him to keep going.

"You don't want a guaranteed A in my class." It's no longer a question. The accusation has disappeared from his voice, leaving a private camaraderie in its place. His tone is musing, instead.

I shake my head, my lips pressed together.

"You don't want more money."

Another shake. Even how much I have feels illicit.

"But you do want to come, sweetheart. Don't try to deny it. I can feel you trembling with how badly you want it."

It's a lie. This time when I shake my head, tears spring to my eyes. Frustration tears. Arousal tears. I'm-in-way-over-my-head tears. I force them back. Force them down, down, down, to that Pandora's box where all my trauma lives.

"It's okay," he murmurs. "Pretend you don't want it."

His kiss is urgent, unyielding. He forces my mouth open, allowing me to feign resistance. Or at the very least, nonchalance. I let him tilt my head back and run his lips down my neck. It's a terrible game I'm playing, letting him take the fall for our mutual destruction.

I should at least tell him, confess my own desire, even if he already knows.

It would be the honorable thing to do.

"Will—"

"Ah ah," he says with a slow shake of his head, with a devastating expression of knowing in his dark eyes. "In this office, you will address me as Professor Stratford."

My secret muscles clench, and he gives me an almost boyish smile.

"This gets you hot, doesn't it, Ms. Hill?"

How is this possible? I had a heavy course load of classes my freshman year, with professors of every shape and size. They were smart and interesting, and for the most part, at least somewhat arrogant. Professor Stratford is all those things…and more. He's simply more. More handsome, more mysterious. More playful as he nips at my lower lip.

"I asked you a direct question, Ms. Hill. Don't make me punish you."

My eyes widen. It's not an entirely fake break in my voice. "What kind of punishment?"

"Let's see," he says, tugging my T-shirt off, leaving me in my bra. The starkness is enough to make my cheeks burn. He's fully clothed while I'm shirtless. "For the first offense, I wouldn't be too harsh. Then again, we can't have disruptive students, can we?"

I thought his fist in my hair had been perverse.

That holding me up against the window had been a wild form of desire.

This is far worse.

And far better.

At least my body thinks so, becoming hot and clenched, swollen around nothing, hungry to have him inside me again, thrusting and thrusting the ache away.

"I tried to behave," I tell him, surrendering to the game. Surrendering to him. "I tried to be a good student. It's just that you were so...distracting."

That earns me a dark chuckle. Large, strong hands undress me with calm expediency, as if stacking books or finding the right page. With both care and anticipation.

At this moment I'm the worn pages of an old

copy of *Romeo and Juliet*.

He thumbs through my pages.

"You'd blame your professor for your own lack of focus?"

I gasp at his touch, low and intimate. It's too much, and I scoot back to get away from him. That only lands me on the edge of his desk, smooth wood cool beneath my bare ass. "Maybe I can make it up to you?"

"Extra credit," he says, musing. "Perhaps an oral report would suffice."

"Please," I whisper.

There's a cruel edge to his smile. "You will give me an analysis on the adaptations of *Romeo and Juliet*, the ones that turn a tragedy into a happy ending."

My eyes widen. Oh. He meant a *real* report. "Like tonight?"

"Like *now*, Ms. Hill. Don't make me lose my patience."

I'm naked on the professor's desk, and he wants me to present a thoughtful commentary. I have the sudden inane thought that maybe this is what the administration meant by advanced literary analysis. "It's wrong."

"Continue."

"It's not what Shakespeare intended."

He drops to his knees in front of me. It should be a weak position, kneeling. Instead he looks formidable, a man who will not be denied. And when he spreads my legs, I sigh with pleasure. "The man is long dead. What does he care?"

Oh God. He's really going to make me think while I'm fully exposed. While he leans close and places a hot, open-mouthed kiss on the inside of my thigh. A whimper escapes. "A-a-authors have... They have dominion...over their work."

He works his way with gentle brushes of his lip until he licks my clit. I nearly jump off the desk, but capable hands hold me down. The sight of them pressing on my skin, the edges of my flesh faintly whitened with the pressure, gives me a warm, shaky feeling inside. Like I'm running through a dark forest. Like I want him to catch me.

He pinches the sensitive skin there, and I squeak.

"Continue," he says, his voice like gravel.

I try not to notice the way he licks his lip, looking at my core in the dusty sunlight as if I'm a feast. I try not to notice, but God, it's the only thing I can see. "Shakespeare had a story to tell. Love it or hate it, but it belongs to him. Not anyone else."

"Isn't every production an adaptation?" he asks. "The actors decide how to read the line. The director decides what to cut and what to keep. Drama has always been interpretive."

Yes, yes, I can see that now. Now that we've had students reading each part in front of the class. Their intonations, their pauses. They all inform the character. I couldn't see it when I sat in a crowded library reading the words on a page. They'd been flat, then.

He licks me from the bottom of my sex to the very tip, to that bundle of nerves. My legs quiver on the wood. I don't know what to do with my hands. I'm waving them in the air like an absolute idiot, flailing, until I do the only thing that makes sense: I put them on his head.

At least it makes sense in the moment before I reach him.

Once I touch his silky-soft hair, such a contrast to the hard line of his jaw, I wonder if this was a mistake. If it's somehow too intimate to feel him this way, my hands pulling at his hair, wanting more, even as his mouth makes me moan. "Not if it obfuscates the entire point."

He looks up with a wicked glint in his eyes. "It obfuscates, does it?"

"Yes, it—"

Another lick, this one so broad I gasp. "What else?"

"It—it bastardizes it."

He sucks at the tender point, making me cry out. My knees try to snap closed, as if to protect myself from too much arousal. Why does it scare me? Except his broad shoulders block the way. As does his stern expression.

Instead, he slowly, carefully, pushes a finger inside me, maintaining eye contact the entire time. I gasp and twitch. He adds another, and it feels too full. Which is strange, because his cock was definitely thicker. Maybe it's the inappropriate setting confusing me.

Then he turns his hand, curves his fingers, and hits a spot that makes my hips press up. My hands fall back to catch my weight on the desk. There's only white-hot sensation.

"What's so wrong with that?" he asks, his tone demanding, almost angry, and for a second, I'm not sure whether he means the adaptation or the pleasure he's giving me. "What's wrong with letting everyone have what they're longing for? He broke the heart of the goddamn world a century ago; why shouldn't we rewrite the story? Why shouldn't we claim it?"

"Because some stories aren't meant to end happily," I cry, and those words feel more real, more like truth, than anything else I've said in this office. "Because the world is still forcing us to grow up too fast, still taking away our choices. It's still making us desperate for a single taste of freedom, and I—" Oh God, his hand is moving faster, fingers fucking me so hard I'm dripping arousal down his wrist.

"Finish it," he growls.

The orgasm or the argument? Maybe both. Maybe I need to say this so I can finally get it out. "I want to know what it feels like to live, even if it's only going to end in tragedy."

"Good," he says, his eyes heavy with arousal, nostrils flared as if he's breathing in my scent. "So fucking good, Ms. Hill. That's what we're doing here. That's what you'll get."

Then he puts his lips to my clit. His fingers are still inside, providing that necessary fullness, that inescapable friction. His warm tongue circles and circles until I'm humping his hand, his face, begging, begging, incoherent, except somehow I hear words: *more* and *please* and *this, this, this is my choice.* My choice no matter how it ends.

Orgasm comes over me in waves. Goose bumps rising on my skin. My nipples turning tight, almost pained. Every muscle in my body locks. I'm fighting it. That's what I realize. I'm fighting the release. Maybe I won't ever reach the summit. Maybe I don't deserve it, anyway. Except I'm not the arbiter. He is. He's the one who judges me, grades me. He's the one who rubs that secret place inside me, and I come with a shattering sensation. I'm spread all over the office, all over campus. I'm in the stars for a brief, almost spiritual moment.

And then, abruptly, it's a hard, flat fall onto earth.

Onto the desk, where I'm slicked with my own desire.

Facing the man who looks smug with masculine pride. He's still panting. "Remember that. Remember that when you go out with Tyler or whoever the fuck else. Remember how it felt when you came on my tongue."

CHAPTER ELEVEN

Dramatic Irony

'M TORN BETWEEN raging hot emotion and numbness through my next two classes.

Eating feels impossible, so I spend lunch checking out a copy of *Romeo and Juliet* from the library, one of many identical copies with a pink textured scroll cover and scrawling old-style font for the title. It's a relatively thin, unassuming package for a story that contains so many deaths. And so much passion. Or is it love? Or is it simply mercurial teenage angst?

Two households, both alike in dignity

Can't believe I had the courage to share my real thoughts in class like that.

I barely ever raise my hand, much less to disagree.

Also can't believe I made out with my professor on his desk.

When I make it back to my dorm, I'm ready to crawl into a dark hole and never leave.

A repairman works on a leak in the roof, the same leak that's been there since last year. Every so often they'll send someone over. It will be proclaimed fixed, only to leak again.

In fair Verona, where we lay our scene

I'm waiting at the elevator when I hear it chug-chug-chugging its way down. It lands with a hard thump and then another for good measure. The old doors squeak open...and stop halfway through. There's enough room for the two people inside to squeeze through the heavy metal doors, but I'm not getting inside.

No telling if they'll open upstairs.

So I take the three flights to my floor, thighs burning, shoulders aching from the weight of my books and laptop in my backpack, eyes gritty from pure stress.

There's a neon green flyer on every single door, including ours.

Comic Sans lettering says something about a meeting.

I ignore it, push inside, and launch myself onto the small bed on the left. The bed is so thin and non-springy that I land with a thud that shakes my brain. I welcome the physical pain as a distraction from the turmoil inside me.

A pair of star-crossed lovers take their life

What kind of play gives away the ending in the opening lines?

That's what I should have stood up and said.

Imagine watching the play for the first time, hearing the ending, but hoping, believing, dreaming that the couple will find their way to a happy ending?

The disappointment is cruel.

Shakespeare should have been locked up for crimes against humanity.

"Bad day?" Daisy asks.

In a two-hundred-square-foot room with two beds and two desks, there isn't exactly room for such luxuries as privacy. We might as well be sitting together on the same park bench, that's how close we are. "It's not so much *bad* as *catastrophic*."

"Did the econ teacher change the textbook again?"

I groan into my pillow. "No, but that's something to worry about for tomorrow."

"Then what happened? The coffee cart stopped serving your hazelnut roast?"

"Okay, no more disaster scenarios, please. I'll tell you. Remember the night at the hotel?"

"The night you made bonkers money? Yeahhh, and you're welcome, by the way."

"For what?" I ask, my voice muffled, only mildly indignant. "I did the work."

"For being the one to suggest it, silly."

"This is what we call in the literary world *dramatic irony*. He's my new professor."

Silence. Then laughter. "You're fucking around."

I peek at her with what I hope is a glare. But it's probably just a pitiful expression. "I'm not fucking around. His full name is Professor William Stratford, and he's teaching Advanced Comparative Analysis of Literature this semester."

Her blue eyes go wide. "You're *not* fucking around."

"Kill me now."

"Unnecessary. You're already dead."

I collapse back onto the bed. "Yeah, that's accurate."

"Did he recognize you?"

"Yes," I say on a growl. "He ordered me into his office after class. Get this. He accused me of doing it *on purpose*, like as some kind of blackmail technique."

Her eyebrows rise. "That's not a bad idea. How much money do you think he'd give you?"

"I'm not blackmailing him. Not for money and not for a good grade."

"Of course you're not blackmailing him for an A. You can already get that for free. Unless…"

"Unless what?"

"Unless he gives you a bad grade because of this."

My blood runs cold. "Why would he do that?"

"I don't know, some kind of pride thing. Men are very sensitive." She frowns. "Or he might do it to discredit you. If a straight-A student tells on him, then he's going to look suspicious. But if that student has a bad grade in his class, it would look more like she's lying just to get out of the class."

"Oh God."

"Maybe you should tell someone."

"Who?"

"I don't know. A counselor? The dean?"

"I promised him I wouldn't."

"This guy might be screwing you over as we speak."

"He wouldn't do that."

She rolls her eyes. "Anne. Don't be naïve. Just because you had sex with a guy once doesn't mean you know him. Or what he'd do to protect himself."

"It wasn't only once."

"What?"

"It was twice. And then... We also made out in his office."

A long groan. "Oh, you're so fucked."

"He said he wrote books. I wonder if I can find them at the library."

I'm already standing when Daisy blocks me at the door. "Anne. I'm doing this for your own good. Don't read his books. Don't look him up on Facebook. If he's going to put this behind him, great. You need to do the same thing."

But what did he write about? Damn it. "Okay. Yes. You're right."

There's a knock from behind her. "Mandatory floor meeting," someone shouts.

"I can't face people right now," I say.

But Daisy drags me to the common area, which contains lumpy cloth couches that have probably held hundreds of students having sex over the years and a small TV that's bolted to the wall to keep people from stealing it.

Everyone looks pink-cheeked and excited with the rush of the first day of classes, their hair windblown from the cold. They lounge on the couches, a few prop themselves on the side table or the bookcase, which groans under the weight.

Daisy and I take our seats cross-legged on the thin carpet in the corner.

A young woman with sharp eyeliner and a plaid skirt taps a clipboard. "Welcome, everyone. I'm Lorelei. My job title is Resident Advisor, got it? I'm not your mother. I'm not your therapist. And I'm not your convenience store if you run out of tampons."

Daisy and I exchange glances. Lovely.

Our last RA mostly left us alone. We didn't tell on her for sleeping with one of the girls on our floor each night. She didn't tell on us for ignoring curfew. The only time she ever yelled at us was when something truly disgusting happened in the bathroom during pledge week.

It seems like this year will be different.

She runs through some of the rules for the bathroom, which are mostly common courtesy. There's only one for the floor which contains a few stalls and a handful of showers. We take our shampoos and razors in little plastic baskets and then back to our rooms.

"It's my job to make sure you're accounted for and in bed by ten p.m."

There's a murmur of dissent through the room.

"Last year it was midnight," someone says.

"Take it up with the university," Lorelei says, clearly unbothered. "If you come in late or not at all, you will be reported to Dormitory Services."

"I'm an adult."

"So am I," she shoots back. "And I'm stuck babysitting you. Don't make me write you up. You'll get in trouble, and I'll be annoyed that you're wasting my time. Dismissed."

She disappears, leaving the rest of us to grumble our discontent.

Not that we really have control over the situation.

We're adults, sure. Adults without full-time jobs or the family money to live in a nice private dorm. Adults who can't get written up without risking their scholarship.

Someone grumbles about getting their parents to write a letter.

Which won't help.

Maybe they'll transfer out, making the line for showers shorter in the mornings.

In the armchair beside Daisy is one of her friends named Alyssa who's in medical school, someone I've met during one of their biology study sessions.

They're the only girls on this floor. The dorm

alternates.

Boys get the ground floor and the third. Girls get the second and fourth.

"What a bitch," Alyssa says.

For some reason, I feel compelled to defend her. "I like her."

Daisy snorts. "For her sparkling personality?"

I shrug. "For her honesty. We're all full of rage and resentment penned up like prisoners or even animals. At least she's not hiding it."

"She does have great winged eyeliner," Daisy says. "I'd ask her for tips if it didn't seem like approaching a baited bear while dripping in honey."

Alyssa grins. "Quite a visual."

"Come on," Daisy says. "I know you've already got a plan. Because no way is my favorite party girl going to be in bed by ten o'clock."

A shrug. "I had a friend who had Lorelei as her RA last year. You just officially sign out, as if you're going home. Easy peasy. No curfew."

"So what about when you're ready to sleep?" I ask. "Do you sneak back in?"

"Past that bulldog?" Alyssa shakes her head. "You just sleep somewhere else. Typically the guy or girl you're hooking up with, as long as they stay in a regular dorm. Or find someone on a floor with an RA who doesn't give a shit who'll let you crash on the floor."

"I once woke up in the library wearing a Cheshire cat onesie," Daisy volunteers. "Campus security doesn't care, really. As long as no one dies."

I shake my head, laughing softly. "Doesn't matter to me, I guess. I don't plan on partying. As long as I can study in my bed, I'm good."

"Are you sure about that?" Alyssa asks, crossing her legs in the armchair even as people filter from the common area back to their rooms. "I have information about a certain exclusive masquerade ball that you might be interested in."

"What is that?" I ask.

"Oh my God," Daisy says. "You got an invite?"

Alyssa grins. "Not yet, but I have hope. I'm sexting with someone on the inside."

I'm lost. "Inside what?"

"The Shakespeare Society," Daisy mutters, covering her mouth as if we're being filmed like Taylor Swift and Selena Gomez at an awards show so no one can lip-read. "It's legendary."

The Shakespeare Society. "Is that a theater troupe or something?"

Daisy and Alyssa break into helpless giggles.

"I guess not." Most of the time I don't really care about being unpopular. I don't have either the time or the inclination to worry about what the popular people are doing. Sometimes, though, I feel like an absolute idiot. Daisy is just as broke as me, just as busy with her classwork, but she still manages to keep up. "Put me out of my misery and tell me."

Alyssa leans over the side of the chair, speaking low even though the room is almost empty. Someone's stretched out on the couch and gently snoring, already asleep at only five o'clock in the evening. "It's a secret society that's super old. Back from when the university was founded or some shit. Really old and prestigious."

"I'm assuming they don't sit around discussing Shakespeare, since there wouldn't be a point to the secrecy otherwise."

"They don't discuss Shakespeare," Daisy says. "They live it."

Alyssa explains. "As legend goes, there was a boy and girl who killed themselves on campus fifty years ago. The secret society was formed after that, like some kind of counterculture movement. There were students and even professors involved."

My eyes widen. "Holy shit."

"I heard they had fancy parties and stunts right under the administrators' noses." Daisy sounds impressed. "But wasn't it disbanded years ago?"

"What kind of stunts?" I ask, frowning.

"Nothing bad," Daisy assures me. "Like they moved that statue of George Washington to the top of the business building. To this day no one knows how they pulled it off. It's just for fun, to blow off steam and keep the university administrators on their toes."

"They disappeared for a few years, but apparently it's ba-ack," Alyssa says in a singsong. "Super secret. Very exclusive. You didn't hear it from me."

"So are you going to try to get in?" Daisy asks.

"Nah, I'm not interested in stealing statues or whatever the hell else they get up to. However, they do have parties where non-members can get invites."

Daisy claps. "Ooh."

"Do you think we'd get in trouble?" I murmur to Daisy.

Her grin is infectious. "Only if we get caught."

We're in the same scholarship program, which has a strict morality clause. Any violations of school rules, including being written up by the dorms or being caught at some illicit party could risk our entire education.

Then again, the idea of belonging to a secret society holds a deep appeal for me.

The kind that doesn't need logic.

The kind that comes from never, ever fitting in.

I can't end up on Professor Stratford's desk again. No matter how good he makes me feel. I need to find a life of my own, belonging of my own. That means being with students, not with professors. Maybe this Shakespeare Society is the key.

Only when it's dark, when I'm staring up at the shapes of old water leaks on the ceiling, does she say from the other side of the small room, "You never told me how it was. The sex."

Warmth floods me before I can stop it, awareness of every nerve ending, the memory of his thickness inside me like a phantom. "Oh. You know. Fine."

"He didn't hurt you?"

Not my body. Maybe my feelings, which is ironic. Giving a huge tip isn't exactly an insult. I'm obviously not cut out to be a sex worker if I was getting a crush on my first night. "He was...nice, actually. I mean, not *nice*. He was filthy and shocking and very, very knowledgeable."

"Really," she says, drawing the word out.

"I never thought I would like something like that, but it also felt like... Oh, it's hard to explain. It finally made *sense*, you know? All the poetry. About passion and intensity and even pain. The way it's all tied up in pleasure. I suppose for someone like me who was curious, it was perfect for the first time."

She sits up in bed, her face lit by the moonlight from the blinds that never quite close. "What the hell do you mean, for the first time?"

"Umm." Shit.

"Why didn't you tell me you were a *virgin*?" Outrage sharpens her voice. It makes the word *virgin* sound like *something I scraped off my shoe*.

"Virginity is a social construct," I say, though the words sound weak.

"You literally just got through telling me about how you felt about it...*as your first time*."

"Okay, maybe it ended up being more real than I thought. It seemed like it didn't matter. It's not like we live in Victorian times where my life is ruined."

She flops on her back with a loud sigh. "I

can't believe you."

"Would you have taken me if you'd known?"

"No. I don't know. But I definitely would have given you more information."

That might have been useful, but I couldn't think about it too hard. I wouldn't have been able to get through it that way. "Why did you assume I *wasn't* a virgin?"

"Aside from the fact that it's the year of our Lord twenty million, and everyone has lost their virginity by sophomore year?" She sounds like she's checking off a list. "And aside from the fact that you are basically a genius and know everything, so why would I assume there's something you *don't* know?"

"I'm actually an idiot. The books are all artifice."

"Says the girl who just used the word *artifice* in a sentence."

"It means pretending to—"

"I know what it means, but the main reason I thought you weren't a virgin is because you told me about Brandon."

Brandon and I dated for a few months. We'd gotten to second base.

Or was it third? I could never remember.

So I'd seen a guy orgasm, even if it was only

by hand.

That was very different from one coming inside me. Very different from one dragging me across a lavish hotel suite by my hair, growling sex words in my ear, making me climax.

"I—I did?"

"About how you didn't mind the kissing part, but then when he got worked up, he got pushy and it was uncomfortable. So I was like, okay, she's having sex with him."

"When he got pushy, I said no. We *didn't* have sex."

"Oh."

The full moon struggles to illuminate even the small room, blocked by ivy and probably a hundred years' worth of grime. It cloaks the room in a soft, silvery glow, which accentuates the weathered features. The small double desk piled high with our supplies. The hanging rack on the door that holds her backpack and my messenger bag.

The sound of stomping from above us breaks the uncomfortable silence.

Then begins a rhythmic thumping of a metal bed frame against the wall. My cheeks heat. Our upstairs dorm-mate is getting lucky tonight. Presumably from someone who lives on the same floor, though perhaps their advisor isn't quite as strict as ours.

"Daisy?"

"Yeah?"

"You know when a guy gets pushy with you, you can say no. Right?"

"Duh," she says, laughing. "Yes. I know. I've read the pamphlets."

We both use the university's health services, which provides doctor's visits and even free tampons. There are giant letters cut out from construction paper on the window, reading *Yes means Yes!* It's a very sex-positive, safe-sex environment.

Despite the quickness of her response, or maybe because of it, worry forms a knot in my stomach. "How was it... You know, for you? With Saul?"

"Are you seriously asking me that?"

"You just asked me that!"

"Because *your* guy turned out to be a super hot professor."

"How do you know he's hot?"

"I looked him up on the university's website. Which you are not allowed to do, by the way. Remember. I'm cutting you off. Cold turkey."

"Saul wasn't *hot*, per se. That doesn't mean it

was bad."

Silence.

The worry turns into full-fledged fear. "Was it really bad?"

More silence.

Now it's my turn to sit up. "Daisy?"

Shuffling of sheets. The squeak of old mattress springs. When she speaks, her voice comes through her pillow. "I don't know."

"Come on. Seriously."

"I *am* being serious. I don't know."

"What... What do you mean, you don't know?"

"I never remember."

"Like when you do the hotel thing?"

"I never remember sex. Ever."

Oh God. I shiver. I knew she came from a scary fundamentalist community, but this feels worse than I thought. What kind of sexual experiences has she had that she...doesn't remember them?

It makes me absurdly grateful that I decided to lose my virginity to a random stranger at the hotel, one who turned out to be experienced with a woman's body, one who knew how to make it good for me.

"Hey, Daisy?"

"Yeah?" Her voice is cautious as if she expects me to pry.

I'm normally awkward and distant, but it feels important. It feels important that she knows she's not alone. "I want you to know that you're my best friend."

She snorts, the sound muffled through the pillow. "Sure, Ms. Knows Carlisle the Pop Princess."

"I'm serious," I say, discomfort making my cheeks heat. "You're my bestie."

A pause. "Yeah?"

"Yeah."

She removes the pillow and looks at me, her blue eyes glinting in the moonlight. Are those tears? I'm afraid to ask. Then she grins. "You're my bestie too."

CHAPTER TWELVE

Rags to Riches

I SHOW UP early on Wednesday to get my own hazelnut blend from the cart with extra sugar, because Lord knows I'm going to need it. I'm determined to make it through this class without embarrassing myself—and without ending up in the professor's office.

That means arriving early enough to stake out the optimal seat.

I spent way too long last night obsessing over where that might be.

The front? So I can show him I'm not bothered?

Or the back, because I am in fact very, very bothered?

Or maybe I pick the same seat in the middle of the class so I don't have to see him scan the room in search of me. Or worse, *not* scan the room in search of me.

I'm also more nervous now that I know his office is right next to the classroom.

The door is closed, the fuzzy glass showing only shadows.

I'm passing by when the door opens. Every cell in my body goes into full-scale panic. I'm about to come face to face with him, except it's not him.

It's…my ex-boyfriend.

He grins when he sees me. "You beat me to it. I was going to get you another coffee."

I try not to show my discomfort on my face. "Brandon."

"I know, I know, we're broken up. I can still buy you coffee, can't I?"

This is getting awkward. "I don't want to lead you on."

"Don't worry," he says, undeterred. "I'm committed to this. To you."

That's what worries me. "I'm not a project."

He gives me a small, slight smile. "You're so sensitive, babe. That's one of the things I like about you, but you gotta know, I'm serious about you."

I struggle to find the words that will push him away without being cruel. "I honestly don't think

I could trust you again after you cheated."

"It wasn't *really* cheating."

Speechlessness holds me to the floor so I don't float away. "What do you mean?"

He lowers his voice. "We weren't having sex yet."

"We were dating. Exclusively."

"Yeah, but we weren't fucking exclusively."

I flinch at the hard word. Fucking. Somehow it's hot when Professor Stratford says filthy things, even degrading things. The difference is that I'm attracted to him. I want him to say those things. "Let's agree to disagree, but either way, there's no future for us. We can be friends."

He puts a hand to his heart. "Friend-zoned. A direct hit."

I manage not to roll my eyes. "If having to be my friend is such a pain, why would you even want to date me?"

He looks around, but even though the hallway bustles with students, some of them entering the classroom, others heading back and forth, no one is pausing long enough to hear us. "You don't understand. Men have needs. It's fine for a girl not to have sex, but for a man it hurts. Like physically hurts."

Take an Advil. That's what I want to retort,

but I don't. "Okay, whatever."

"And you're a virgin," he continues, "which I understand. You weren't ready."

Oh God. "I'd really rather not talk to you about this."

"I have some ideas about how we can make you ready."

My eyes close. It was embarrassing enough to talk about this in a private hotel suite. Or in the back of Brandon's hand-me-down BMW, where I first confessed it to him.

I never wanted to sleep with anyone at Port Lavaca, where people muttered *white trash* when I passed by. Not that I had time to really date between high school, working part-time at the diner, and cleaning the house.

Brandon might not even have met me at a university this large. He lives off campus in the most prestigious frat house and is majoring in business. But we had the same minimum science requirement. Chemistry had been interesting enough. More fun than the high school version, anyway. Though I'm glad it's not my major.

We'd ended up lab partners. I'd done our work, and he'd asked me out.

It had felt nice to be pursued. To belong somewhere, even if it was only a frat party, even if

I was only invited because my boyfriend was a member.

So I agreed to one date.

Then another.

It's not that we never kissed. We made out plenty of times in the back seat of his car, his panting steaming up the windows, while I tried to get into it. Or at least pretend. Something had kept me from going all the way, from losing my virginity to him.

It's not that I was precious about it. It's just a social construct, the way I told Will.

I mean, the way I told Professor Stratford.

But something held me back.

I never felt that aroused when he touched me. I thought maybe it was just me, maybe I wasn't interested in sex. That night in Cressida City proved that wrong. I'm a highly sexual creature...as long as I'm with an older man who quotes Shakespeare and pulls my hair.

"We just never had a bed, that's the problem. We always tried it in the back seat, where it's impossible to get comfortable. And you always have that weird roommate around."

"A BMW is more comfortable than most beds. And Daisy is not weird."

"She comes from a cult."

My hackles rise to my friend's defense, even if he's kind of right. She's not the reason we never had sex. "She comes from a fundamentalist religious community, which may or may not be a cult, but where she comes from doesn't define her."

"And I know the guys at my frat house make you uncomfortable. They're assholes, anyway. So I was thinking I could get us a hotel room on the weekend."

Oh God. Why is saying *no* so incredibly difficult? I feel like I've already rejected him a bunch of different ways, but it doesn't seem to be working. Part of me knows it's not my job to make him understand, that he should respect my boundaries which have already been stated clearly, even if I were still a virgin.

The other part of me is just desperate to make this end.

"I slept with someone," I whisper.

Emotions cross his boyish face. Surprise. Then a flush of telling anger. Jealousy. "Are you serious? We were only broken up over the summer. I thought you were working."

It's too much. "I *was* working, not that it's any of your business after you cheated. And then managed to sleep around so much that I heard about it. And you slept with a lot more than one person. More than one person at a time, if the rumors are to be believed."

That's how I found out about his cheating.

Tanglewood Tea is a social media account that details gossip on campus, from affairs between professors to students getting expelled to antics of the football team. They use investigative reporting and tips as their sources. No one knows who's really behind it. It's been going for years, so there are rumors that it's passed down as people graduate. Or it could even be run by someone on the faculty.

But I owe that person my thanks, because they posted blurry images of him getting a blow job from not one but two different girls. They'd been blurred out, even their clothes to make it hard to identify them, but his face in the throes of pleasure had been unmistakable. *Golden Boy Enjoying Summer in Ibiza; Does GF know?*

Girlfriend did not know.

He narrows his eyes. "I swear to God, if I find out who was behind that account…"

"You'd what? They were only telling the truth."

"They had no fucking business following me around. My mother's lawyer sent a cease and desist, but they refuse to take it down."

"You're more concerned with people knowing that you cheated than you are about the fact that you actually cheated." I sigh, because he can't help who he is. But this conversation isn't going anywhere. "The fact is that you and I never really had anything in common. Our sex lives were just a reflection of everything else."

"Who did it?"

"What?"

"Who took your virginity?" He frowns, looking thoughtful. And pissed off. "Was it Jake? I knew that bastard was sniffing around your heels. He likes taking my castoffs."

"Your *castoffs?*"

"Or is it one of your pretty boy poetry majors?"

"You'll never know," I snap.

"I can't believe this." He has the balls to act offended. "Sex means nothing, you know that? It's just a physical need like eating or sleeping. But you and me as a couple? With my political plans and your little rags-to-riches story? We could've gone all the way."

My little rags-to-riches story.

It feels like the breath has been knocked out of my lungs.

"Are you serious?" I manage. "I'm not rich." That's not my biggest complaint about the phrase. It's more the derision that bothers me, the reduction of a lifetime of struggling into a neat little PR-friendly soundbite, but it's what comes out.

"Do you need money?" he asks. "I could help you out. You know that."

That's when the door to Professor Stratford's office opens. Not the one that goes directly into the classroom. The one that goes to the hallway where we're standing. The crowd has thinned as we've gotten close to the start time. Someone passes by with their head down, headphones in, but we're virtually alone, the three of us.

"What's going on out here?" Professor Stratford asks.

Panic pricks every inch of my body. "Nothing."

He peruses me with deep interest, his dark gaze taking in my tense stance, my messenger bag clutched to my chest like a shield, the anxiety I'm barely holding back. He turns to Brandon, who shifts his weight, trying to look innocent but with defiance coming through.

"Brandon?" he asks, his voice low.

I hadn't realized he would know him. After

all, Professor Stratford is new to campus. And he teaches an advanced class in the humanities department, something Brandon doesn't need to take as part of his MBA track program.

"Talking to my girlfriend," Brandon says, his voice tight. "Or do you have a problem with that? Maybe you'd like to get a transcript of our conversation."

My eyes widen. That's a super intense way to speak to a professor, especially one who did nothing more than step outside his own office. And it sounds weirdly...personal. "We're not...um... We're not dating anymore."

Brandon glares at me, even more pissed off with an audience. "Maybe we would be if you hadn't gone and slept with—"

An involuntary squeak escapes me.

The man I slept with is standing right beside us, watching us with too-perceptive eyes. "Do you need assistance, Ms. Hill?"

"No, thank you. I'm done talking with him." I turn to Brandon. "Please leave."

My ex-boyfriend gets a sulky expression. "I didn't mean to get so mad, Annie. It just took me by surprise, that's all. Let's meet up after class."

"She asked you to go," comes Professor Stratford's voice, silky with threat.

Brandon doesn't seem to recognize the danger. "I'm an adult now, Dad. You can't tell me what to do anymore. You can't send me to my room or ground me."

For a second, a sweet second, I think it's a joke. The way Daisy rolled her eyes and said, *okay, Mom*, when I asked her to put her seat belt on in the cab ride over to the hotel.

For that second, I can believe that these two men, my past and present, my ex-boyfriend and my one-night stand, aren't related to each other.

Blissful ignorance.

And then time marches on, impervious to my blooming horror.

Because Brandon looks very serious about the word *Dad*, and Professor Stratford seems to accept it. As if it's the truth. As if they're really related that way.

"We'll talk about this later," Professor Stratford says, a warning glint in his eyes. "I suggest you find your own classroom, which is on the other side of campus."

They maintain fierce eye contact while I struggle not to faint.

Holy shit.

Then Brandon leaves without another word to me, without even glancing my way.

Professor Stratford curses when he looks at me.

He pulls me into his office, and I stumble alone, barely able to stay conscious. What's happening to me? He sits me down in a rolling leather chair that's still faintly warm from his body. His strong hand goes to the back of my neck. He pushes down so my head is almost between my knees. My messenger bag has slipped to the floor.

"Breathe," he orders.

I can't, but I also can't speak. Instead I make a choking sound.

His hand rubs gentle, impossibly slow circles on my back. "You can do it, sweetheart. Take a deep breath in. Let the air inside."

After a long, painful burn I finally gasp in a breath.

"Good girl," he says, approving. "Another one."

I manage to take another breath, this one shaky, but I'm getting the hang of it now. "What was that?" I gasp, my voice a faint rasp in the privacy of his office. The same office that he kissed me in only two days ago.

"A panic attack. Have you had one before?"

My head shakes. I close my eyes. "I didn't

know…"

"Didn't know that Brandon was my son?" He sounds sympathetic, and also faintly sardonic, resigned to his fate. "We skipped the getting-to-know-you phase, you and I."

I finally sit up, facing him. "His last name isn't Stratford."

"He has his mother's last name."

"Why?" The truth is that's none of my business, how they pass down names in their family. I'm so busy being stunned that words just fall out of my mouth. As if anything he could explain would take away the terrible shock.

"It's complicated. His mother's family is something of a dynasty."

His mother's family, which means that Professor Stratford had a child with another woman. He was probably married to her. Oh God, what if he's still married? "The Baldwin Building," I say, remembering his pride when we walked past it.

"Named after his grandmother." He notices me looking at his left hand, which is bare. "I'm not married. I wouldn't cheat on my wife."

The words *my wife* make me flinch.

And they bring back the memory of Brandon's ludicrous idea that we would somehow be a long-term couple based on my little rags-to-riches story. Not that I have riches. Not compared to the kind of money that can put names on buildings.

I have the money that Professor Stratford gave me.

"It doesn't matter," I tell him, even though it feels like a big weight off my shoulders. "Even if you did cheat, that would be on you. Not me."

"That's true," he says. "It's also true that it's none of my damn business what you do with anyone...even Brandon. But I have to ask. How long did you date?"

My cheeks turn warm. "It was a few months."

"Why did you break up?"

Hell. I wonder if I'll get in trouble for answering. "He cheated on me."

His eyes narrow. "Fuck. I'm sorry."

"It's not your fault. Or maybe it is, for not raising him better than that." I force a laugh, though it sounds slightly manic. "It's weird to be talking about this with his father. And even weirder to be talking about it with my professor."

He frowns. "There's more to say, but class has already started."

I press the back of my hand to my forehead, forcing calm. "I'm fine, okay?"

He sighs, looking torn. "Let's go."

We leave the office at the same time, from

opposite doors. He goes straight into the classroom. I hear his low voice booming through the old walls, even if I can't make out the words. I exit into the hallway, counting to five before slipping into the classroom with my head down as if I'm just randomly late instead of having an existential sex crisis.

Most of the seats on this side of the classroom are taken, but Tyler waves at me. He points down at the seat next to him as he lifts his backpack where he'd clearly been saving a seat. If I want to take one of the other seats in the far back, I'd have to walk across the front of the room in front of everyone. And hurt Tyler's feelings.

So I attempt a smile of thanks and sit down next to him.

"Today we're going to talk about Paris," Professor Stratford says. "Who is he?"

"A perv," someone says, and everyone laughs. It's not a rebellious type of laughter but a relaxed one. Everyone's ready to dive into the discussion after the last class.

"Why's that?" Professor Stratford asks.

"Because he wants to marry someone who's so young."

A dark eyebrow rises. "And how do we know how old he is?"

"The text doesn't say," a girl in the front seat says. "But we know that he's a member of the ruling House of Verona. So he's probably at least in his late twenties, maybe thirties."

Professor Stratford nods. "Inference. That's an important tool in analysis. What else do we know about him, aside from his possible perv status?"

I raise my hand but don't wait for him to call on me before speaking. No one else is, and I have a sinking feeling he's not going to call on me to read this time either. Why doesn't he want me in front of the class? Does he think I'd do a bad job? "He's traditional," I say, which causes the other students to quiet down. "He wants to marry her because it will be a good match, not because he cares about her or even knows her."

Approval shines in his dark eyes, and I hear the words he murmured to me in the office only a few minutes ago. *Good girl.* "That's right. Back then it was common enough to have marriages for political or dynastic purposes."

He opens a discussion of whether we still have those, and people bring up celebrity marriages that are said to have been PR stunts. The whole while we hold eye contact, up until the moment he pulls out his battered copy of *Romeo and Juliet* to continue the readings.

My phone vibrates. I pull it out. There's only a link.

I click on it before realizing I'm probably downloading some kind of spam bot. Except that's not what opens. Instead it's a black website with white text that looks like hand-written scroll. *The Shakespeare Society presents a masquerade ball. Bring a friend and leave your inhibitions behind...* It lists Saturday night at eight o'clock, along with a set of coordinates that I presume are the location. I swallow hard, fighting back excitement.

Part of me wants to ignore this invitation. It's probably dangerous.

Definitely against the rules.

And I prefer to follow the rules.

Tell no one under pain of death. I hope the threat isn't literal...

It's a joke, right?

The idea of belonging to something feels so, so good. Being a part of something larger than myself. Isn't that why I wanted to come to Tanglewood University?

Isn't that why I fought so hard to leave home?

Professor Stratford's dark gaze meets mine, mysterious and aloof. He represents everything I can't have, all the places I don't belong. Except I was just invited somewhere. Invited somewhere he definitely won't be.

CHAPTER THIRTEEN

Downright Genial

G OING HOME MAKES me feel guilty.

It's like the jail tile on Monopoly. You know you're just visiting, but it still feels scary, as if the bars might close in on you while you're there.

As if you might get trapped.

Our house is south and east of Tanglewood. Far enough away that some people have never even visited there. It's a little less than a two-hour drive, but it feels like a world away.

This all used to be farmland. I still pass rows of dark-colored corn stalks in the old bus that takes me there, that smell of manure a grim reminder of where I'm going. That ends before we get home, though. These were plantations, way back when. Over the years, the land was split into parcels and sold off, one by one, as those wealthy families fell on hard times. Now the white antebellum mansions are often derelict with rotting interiors and missing windows, black spaces in a creepy old smile.

The bus leaves me at the Stop N' Low, where I wave to Mr. Williams.

I'm the only one getting off here.

Most of the sleepy passengers travel on.

The off-brand convenience store serves as more than the gas station. They have a laundromat, check cashing and notary, a café that sells hamburgers and Chinese food. Mrs. Williams does tarot readings in the back room.

In comparison with other stores in town, business is booming.

It takes me thirty minutes even cutting through the old, abandoned orchard. Rotting apples dot the mud. A few small, overripe fruits hang heavy on the limbs. No one has worked this land for as long as I can remember, which makes the continued harvest a small miracle.

No one really farms around here, anymore.

Our land is in the shape of a long, uneven triangle.

One time Dad got the idea to try his hand at growing things. In the far corner you can still find little fists of potatoes dug up by rodents. They gnaw through the skin to the white starch beneath and then leave the rest behind. The potatoes aren't even good enough for the wild animals to eat.

I step over the drooping metal gate and walk the gravel path to the house. The lawn is scattered with weeds and broken-down cars that Dad swears he's going to fix up and sell.

The space beneath the carport is filled with more junk that one day could be our fortune. I step around a pile that includes all things metal: tools, barbells, scraps. And trip over a piece of plywood that's come loose from the discarded lumber stack.

The familiar sight of our kitchen door, white with scuff marks and a dingy yellow curtain, makes my stomach clench. I peek inside with more fear than I'd like to admit. The sink overflows with dirty dishes. Dirty pots and pans crowd the stovetop. The round table holds mountains of mail along with more used dishes. Flies work their way lazily from plate to plate, secure in their safety. It's gross but also a relief. Because my dad isn't here.

I creep through the rest of the house but find only more trash.

A cockroach skitters in front of me.

When I make it to the bedroom and peek inside, I sigh. Only my mother is inside, sitting up in the bed, covered in the faded blue comforter. The light from the TV throws bluish light on her pale skin. Her eyes brighten when she sees me. "Annie!"

I step over piles of clothes and give her a hug. "I'm not hurting you, am I?"

"No, Annie-girl. You could never hurt me."

I'm still gentle as I smooth her greasy hair back. "Do you want me to help you shower?"

"Maybe later."

"I can't stay too long this time. I have a...a study group tonight."

She pats the worn sheets beside her. "Come here and tell me all about that fancy school of yours and your new classes and people who study on a Saturday night."

She always says she's fine, but I know how fragile her health can be. I'm careful to keep my weight from rolling her as I sit beside her. "They started Monday."

"Who's your favorite professor?"

Christ. The question brings Professor Will Stratford's image to mind before I can stop it. His handsome face. I don't even see him the way he looked in class, all serious and formal. No, my mind conjures up the version of him flushed from kissing me, dark eyes heavy with lust.

I still can't quite comprehend him being Brandon's father.

They don't particularly look alike.

Professor Stratford has dark hair and dark eyes and a mouth that makes me think sinful thoughts. Like him kneeling between my legs, mouth slick from my arousal.

Brandon has dirty-blond hair and brown eyes, which I suppose he got from his mother.

"My economics professor," I say, lying so hard that God should strike me with lightning. "She was the economic advisor for a former president."

My mom whistles. "And she's teaching you about budgeting?"

"Not exactly." Though knowing how to budget would be helpful. Assuming I actually had money. The remainder of the cash is tucked into my pocket, burning a hole. "More like inflation. Supply and demand. Unfair competition."

"I thought you wanted to read about poetry and stuff."

"You know how it is in the beginning. They mostly cover the syllabus and expectations." Except Professor Stratford hadn't done that. There wasn't even a syllabus. Just lectures. Exactly what my dream class would have been. If it hadn't been taught by him. I both want him and hate him, desire him and fear him. We don't belong together on any level—not class or education or age. It's only some perverse feeling inside that makes me long for him.

Being home reminds me why that can never happen.

He's obviously at home in opulence and academic privilege.

I come from filth. Literally.

A long sigh. "We've needed you here."

My heart clenches. "I'm here now," I say, too bright. "How about I start cleaning up and then later we can watch a show together?"

Her gaze shifts around the room. She won't meet my eyes.

"Mom?"

"It's your father." She shakes her head. "He's been gambling again."

My blood runs cold. "But he was doing so well."

"I know, but that damn gambling friend of his came around again."

"That's *not* his friend, Mom. That's his bookie."

"Well, you know your father. He means well.

He tries his very best, but he can't keep up with it. Addiction is a disease, you know. It's not his fault."

"If it's a disease, then he needs treatment."

She puts her hands up. "What can we do?"

I really didn't know. That was the problem. Addiction may be a disease, like the cancer riddling my mother's body, but I couldn't fix it. I couldn't fix either illness. "We don't have any money. We're already in debt to the hospital. What if they don't let you go anymore?"

"It's worse than that," she admits.

My stomach sinks. "How much worse?"

"They might take the truck."

"Oh God."

"I don't know how he'll go to work. And then we'll have even less money."

"What about your doctor's visits?"

"Those won't happen either."

"What are we going to do?"

Mom shakes her head, looking sad. "It would help if you didn't go to that fancy school, if you worked full-time at the diner. We would have more money then."

"I can't," I whisper through numb lips.

I can't because it wouldn't even be living. It would be giving up.

Professor Stratford may be forbidden, but I can have Tanglewood University. I can have the Hathaway Dormitory and my friends and maybe even the Shakespeare Society. If I can finish cleaning in time to make the last bus back to the city.

The familiar sound of the truck rumbles outside.

A door slams and then my father enters the room, carrying a big brown paper bag.

"My two favorite girls." My father's followed by a big brown-and-white dog, his fur dappled with spots. Rusty gives me a pleased squint as he comes over for some pets.

"Hi," I mumble, unable to meet his eyes. He'd see my anger. Instead I focus on the old dog, giving him a good rubdown as he pushes the top of his butt into my hands.

"Why the long faces?" Dad asks.

Mom gives my arm a warning squeeze. She doesn't want me to talk about money. Even if it's going to lose the truck, even if it's going to lose our only form of transportation to get her to the doctor so she can have treatment.

I force myself to smile. "I was just telling her about my new classes."

"Already boring you to death?" he asks with a

laugh. "I don't know how you stand it, honestly. Who needs books when you have a TV with unlimited streaming?"

I grit my teeth together because I've heard this a hundred times.

As a child they berated me for being unsociable, for being reclusive. Because I wanted to read a book in my room instead of sitting and watching endless hours of TV with them. It's always on even when no one is watching it even when no one is home.

The blue light of strangers is always in the room.

"I really like my new comparative analysis class," I say, somewhat defensively.

It's only after the words are out of my mouth that I realize I've opened up a particular pathway. Obviously I'm not going to tell them about that evening at the hotel. Or the unfortunate turnabout that the man was my professor.

I don't ever tell them about my money problems.

They didn't know I was struggling to get the economics textbook. And they sure as hell don't know that I had sex with a man, with my professor, in order to buy it. They think my scholarship includes it or maybe they never wonder at all. And I have no reason to tell them otherwise. It would just make them worry.

And complain about the fact that I'm in college.

They don't see the point.

"Comparative analysis," my dad says. "Hmm."

"Now, Richard," my mom says, her voice trilling. "We're going to support our little girl's dreams, even if they're a hardship to us."

"You're absolutely right, Debra." He looks repentant but in an exaggerated way.

A performative way.

As if he's an actor on a stage.

"We're studying Shakespeare," I offer, my voice small. I hate that I get this way at home, but I can't seem to help it. Capable, determined Anne Hill, sophomore at Tanglewood University, on the dean's list, disappears. In her place is little helpless Annie trapped in a filthy house with our heat and water turned off. "The professor is having us read the lines in front of the class, almost like a play is being acted out. It's kind of like a TV show."

My father gives a great big belly laugh. "Without any special effects?"

I force a laugh to match him and my mother.

"Right."

"Of course, your mom likes those reality shows. They don't have no special effects." He frowns, as if pondering their value. Then he brightens. "Of course, they're *real*."

A wince doesn't escape me. It doesn't matter that reality shows are often scripted. Or at the very least, carefully crafted and curated for our entertainment. That's exactly what Shakespeare and other playwrights did at the Globe, the famous playhouse in London.

It would be fun to examine it with Professor Stratford, actually, the rapid development of TV shows for public entertainment to the old playwrights, the use of high-stakes themes to draw interest, the use of so-called drama and gossip to convey powerful emotional arcs.

It would be a fun exercise, if I could meet him without thinking of sex.

My father's already moved on. "Yep, always supported our little girl even though she has the strangest ideas sometimes. Remember those ballet classes when she was a little girl? As if our clumsy child could have been a prima ballerina?"

My mother laughs heartily, not realizing the insult.

Or maybe she does realize it.

Maybe that's what's funny.

I force my expression to be blank. It's something I have a lot of practice with.

When people look at terrible homes and wonder why the children don't always look distressed… It's because we learn to hide it. It's easier that way. Less chance of being punished for daring to contradict. My parents aren't the most violent in Port Lavaca. In fact most of the time they're downright genial. As long as you don't challenge them.

The ballet class he's referring to was a free class at the local community center. They'd sold a cheap set of beginner leotards, tights, and pointe shoes. My parents balked at paying anything, so I'd had to show up in my sneakers and jeans.

I still remember the pity on the teacher's face.

She let me join in without comment.

Next season I told my parents I didn't want to do ballet.

But that wasn't it.

Sure, I'd never have become a prima ballerina, but that wasn't really the point. It was art. It was expression. The real reason I didn't want to go back was so that I wouldn't have to see the pity. Even the other parents looked sorry for me.

I didn't want to be mocked by the other girls.

Because I would never fit in with everyone else.

Even at Tanglewood I haven't fit in. People know I'm the scholarship kid, the one who lives at Hathaway Dormitory. Except now that I'm going to the Shakespeare Society's masquerade ball, maybe things will be different.

Maybe I'll find my people there.

I force a bright tone. "I was just telling Mom that we could watch a show together."

"Will you have time to clean up?" My dad looks worried. "We're just not able to keep up with it all without you. You know that, Annie-bear."

"Of course," I say, because it needs to be done. And maybe it feels good to have them need me, even if it's only to clean up. "I'll focus on cleaning before I go."

"Good, good." He lifts the grease-stained brown paper bag. "I brought dinner."

My stomach turns over. I can already smell that it's something heavily fried inside. That can't be good for her while her body is recovering.

"I can cook you something," I murmur.

Mom laughs. "Don't be silly, darling. The fridge went out last week."

Great.

The next six hours disappear in a whirl of scrubbing, vacuuming, and washing.

I tackle the dishes first, drawing a sink full of soapy water and scrubbing each dish of its dried food until everything is stacked and gleaming. Then I work on the kitchen table, throwing out trash bags full of mail and fast-food wrappers.

Only then do I gather up the courage to open the fridge.

The putrid puff of warm air makes me gag.

I tie a handkerchief around my face while I empty everything liquid into the sink and everything else into trash bags. A large pile of bags forms a mountain by the front door.

Once that's done, I move on to the living room, clearing more food wrappers, picking up dirty clothes, and doing laundry. At least the washing machine and dryer haven't gone out.

When the floor is finally cleared, I grab the vacuum.

Fleas are caught through the bristles. They land in the dirt container, made of clear plastic, so I can see them hopping around. I take the vacuum all the way outside before opening it and dumping everything, both filth and fleas, into a bag so the fleas can't get back out.

It's a grim death for them.

I feel a little guilty about it but not enough to stop.

I have some pesticide powder I can spray on the carpet before I go.

Not that it will help much with such a thriving population.

Other kids had bicycles and Barbies.

I spent my time picking fleas off my clothes. There were always red bumps on my skin, particularly around my ankles. They could reach me there even when I walked around.

Poor Rusty has it the hardest though. He can barely move without having to sit and scratch himself. Which is why I give him a bath using flea shampoo I picked up at the store.

I scrub him really good, pulling the tiny black insects with my fingers.

It's disgusting but then that's nothing new.

Between the smell of fried chicken and French fries wafting from the bedroom and my tasks, my stomach threatens to upchuck. Good thing I planned ahead and didn't eat breakfast.

It's better now.

Better because I have a dorm that I can go to after I'm done. A place that's clean. A place that's my own. It's better because I actually can buy my own cleaning supplies. We barely ever had them when I was younger. A dried old sponge and water doesn't do much to combat filth, though. My parents don't seem to mind much. They ask me to clean up, sure, but even when I'm away at school they don't step in.

I can still hear Professor Stratford's low voice at the hotel.

So I must conclude that you are Cinderella.

I think I'd prefer being covered in ashes to fleas, but I didn't get to pick.

When everywhere else is done, I move to the master bedroom. Mom sits up in bed along with Dad. They've mostly finished eating, the dregs of fried foods sprinkling the bedspread. Some dating show is on the TV. I step across their field of vision quickly so they don't complain.

My phone buzzes in my pocket.

It's Daisy. *Where the hell are you?*

Taking longer than I thought, I text back, shuddering at the memory of the fridge. The scent is permanently burned into my nose. The idea of a masquerade ball feels so far removed from how filthy I feel right now. Do I even deserve to go?

She sends me an eye-rolling emoji. *Get your ass back here.*

I bite my lip. I don't belong at some fancy masquerade ball any more than I belong at the hotel. This is where I am. This is *who* I am. *You can go without me,* I type.

I shove the phone back in my pocket despite the series of poop and bomb emojis that come in. The phone vibrates in my pocket, but I continue ignoring it.

"Who's that?" my mom asks.

"My roommate," I say, pocketing my phone.

"What was her name again? Dolores? Dorothy?"

"Daisy."

"Like the flower?" My dad snorts. "Who would name their kid after a flower?"

I don't point out that my name is probably the most boring name in the history of the world. He manages to complain and insult people with such a jolly affect that people often don't get it. At least, when they first meet him. After a lifetime in Port Lavaca, most people just ignore him. Because despite that cheerful veneer, there's a temper underneath.

More than anyone else, I know not to tempt it.

When the house is sparkling, or at least the best I can do, I drag the trash bags down the long gravel driveway one by one. I'm sweating and overheated and gross. The cool breeze outside feels amazing. I let myself fall onto the gravel on my back. I close my eyes against the bright sunlight hoping the heat will burn away all the germs, the filth, the memories.

Sometimes when I'm in my dorm room, I wake up from a nightmare.

Where I'm covered in trash, surrounded by overfilled trash bags, covered in grime.

I remind myself that I don't have to live like that anymore.

But you do, whispers a voice inside me.

Of course I can't abandon my parents, especially with my mother being sick.

Which means I'm doomed to clean this place again and again.

My very own boulder up a hill.

Rusty pads across the gravel driveway and licks my face until I laugh, pretending not to notice the salty tears at the corners of my eyes that he licks away.

Because I don't cry. I never do.

CHAPTER FOURTEEN

Masquerade Ball

I MISS THE last bus back to Tanglewood for the day, which means I'm missing the masquerade ball. Missing out on being part of something fun and interesting.

Missing out on my chance at belonging.

But I can't stand the smell even after hours of cleaning, can't stand the callous laughter.

I can't even stand Rusty's trusting eyes. He doesn't understand that he shouldn't have to be covered in fleas.

He isn't even mad about it.

Maybe I would be a happier person if I could learn to be like him, content with my lot in life, taking whatever scraps of affection are thrown my way, but I just can't.

To my parents' disappointment, I never could.

No. I refuse to miss the masquerade ball.

So I do the only thing I can do to get back in time.

I spend some of my nest egg to splurge for a cab back to school.

When I get back to the dorm, I spend a long time showering, lathering my body twice and washing my hair three times, making sure I'm completely clean. Wearing only a towel wrapped around me and my slippers, I push open the door to the dorm room—and squeak in surprise.

"Ta-da!" Daisy stands in the middle of the room doing jazz hands.

There's a sparkly black dress on my bed and strappy heels on the floor.

"What's this?" I ask, holding the towel tighter around me.

"Well, I was doing a risk/benefit analysis of driving all the way to Port Lavaca to pick you up, but then I looked at your location on the map, and you were heading home."

Home. Yes, the dorm is home now. Not where I spent the day. "Stalker."

She grins. We shared our locations with each other early in our roommate experience, so that if one of us ever goes missing, the other can find them. That was more so that I could find Daisy, not the other way around. "As if I would go without you. It's your invitation."

"I don't think they'll be checking names at a masked ball."

"Fair point, but I wouldn't go without you because we're friends."

"Aww, how sweet," I say, my voice dry, because I don't know how to handle actual affection between friends. "What about this whole curfew thing?"

"We both checked out for the weekend," she reminds us. "As long as Lorelei the Demon Resident Advisor doesn't notice us sneaking out, she'll assume we're still off campus. And I have a friend who's going to let us crash at their private dorm."

I look at the dress on my bed and swallow hard. What if campus administrators get mad about it? But right at this moment, I'm desperate to feel something other than cold despair. That's how I end up on campus in the chilly evening, whispering to Daisy. The sign above the wide doors reads *Baldwin Building.*

"Are they allowed to have an event here?" I whisper.

"Of course not. That's what makes it fun."

"Oh God." But I can't deny the thrill of excitement in my veins.

She knocks three times on a side door, and after a moment, it opens. The guy looks a little older than the average student. He's wearing a suit and…an earpiece? He looks as if he should be security at some kind of congressional event.

This is *not* a random frat party.

We're shown a selection of masks at the entry.

I choose one that's all black with glitter because it matches my dress.

And because it's way less showy than the other bright colors and wild plumes of feathers. I'm trying to dip my toe into the water, not dive into the deep end. Daisy digs through the large felt container and finds one made of gold filigree with an asymmetrical design flaring on the left. It looks gorgeous with her red slinky dress, as if she's a ruby on a pure gold chain. In contrast I'm a bit like the night, the hint of glitter like a puddle glinting moonlight.

We're shown down a stairwell with rough metal and rubber steps. "What is this place?" I whisper. "I didn't even know it had a basement."

"It's a bomb shelter," she whispers. "We have them in the engineering building. Which is a nice bonus."

"How so?" I ask, keeping my balance on the

heels with my palm on the concrete wall.

"You know. If the world ends, we'll still be alive down here."

I snort. "And end up eating glitter and frat boys to survive."

"That's dark," she says, giggling.

A black curtain divides the steps from...everything else. Sound and energy beats through heavy velvet. Daisy pushes through, and we're immersed in another world. It doesn't seem industrial like I thought it would be. Or abandoned. Instead there's lush seating and cocktails, a bar with a tall wall of amber liquids behind it. A DJ plays music in the next large room, the bass reverberating through thick rugs beneath us.

"Holy shit," I say.

Daisy claps. "This is perfection."

I turn in a slow circle, peering into another large room where a bank of poker tables and roulette wheels gather people in groups. "I'm still terrified of being caught, but...damn, I'm glad I came back, just so I could see it. It's like some kind of fever dream."

"Let's get a drink," she says, not waiting for me as she heads to the bar.

The drinks menu has more than just alcohol. There are options that specify milligrams of THC in liquid form, ecstasy, and acronyms I don't even know.

"There are no prices," I say, flipping the black menu. There's nothing more except for a symbol embossed into the leather, a hand holding a skull. Probably a reference to the gravedigger scene in *Hamlet*. A moment of comedy in an otherwise tragic tale.

"There's no cash register, either," she says, glancing around.

"You don't pay for anything," someone shouts from the stool next to us.

Holy shit again. They're giving out drinks and recreational drugs for free? "Where does the Shakespeare Society get their money?"

A shout of laughter. "Girl Scout Cookies."

If Daisy is a ruby on a gold chain, we're in a veritable jewelry box.

Women are wearing dresses nicer than I've ever seen in a variety of beautiful colors and styles—a deep violet ball gown complete with a hoop skirt, an actual pale pink tulle tutu paired with what can only be a black bikini top, a super short azure silk slip and five-inch heels.

The men mostly wear slacks and dress shirts, some of them white but more of them in jewel tones. A few of them sport bespoke suits in leopard-spotted velour or corduroy with exaggerated stitching. Someone is wearing a mask of a horse, not speaking, only making neigh sounds. It's shocking, intimidating, but also a delight to the senses.

It's art.

And like all art, it doesn't need a purpose. Only to surprise and delight. Only to make us feel something, even for a few moments. I'm a million light years away from my house in Port Lavaca, and I'm grateful for the ride.

"I've never seen anything like this," I say. "Have you?"

Daisy breathes a laugh. "My family's idea of a good time is sitting around talking about all the reasons why God is mad at you and you're going to hell."

The bartender comes over, and my eyes widen when I realize it's the same one from the hotel. The one with dark hair falling into his eyes like he's a young man at a Renaissance salon, spouting poetry with Lord Byron. The one wearing a plain white shirt and black hipster suspenders.

He winks. "What'll it be, ladies?"

Daisy looks at me, her eyebrows raised.

"Umm." I glance back at the menu. "Can I get the Midsummer Night's Dream?"

"Any toppers?"

The toppers are what they call the drugs. "No, thank you."

He looks at Daisy. "And for you?"

"Water, please."

"What?" I ask, exasperated. "If I ordered that, you'd give me a hard time."

"Only because you usually order water. I *don't* usually order water, making this a novel and exciting experience. Will it taste like minerals? Will there be ice?"

Her gentle taunts don't fool me. "What's wrong?"

She focuses very hard on her ascent to the leather and black metal barstool as if it takes all her concentration. That way I can't see her eyes. I take the seat next to her, but I don't say anything. I can wait her out. Which she knows.

"I went home," she murmurs. "Like you."

My heart clenches. "You didn't tell me."

"It was a last-minute thing. You packed your bags and left, and I thought...why not?"

I withhold my groan. It's not like I'm in a position to judge. Both of us come back from our home visits feeling completely defeated. It begs the question of why we continue to return.

She runs her fingers over the smooth bar top,

tapping in rapid anxiety, Morse code for *this is my nightmare.* "You know I'm one of five girls. The youngest. The only one not married."

In fact I know that most of them got married under the age of eighteen to men their father chose and now have multiple babies of their own. "Mhmm."

"This," she says, waving a hand around, gesturing not only at the party but all of Tanglewood University. The entire life she leads. A life of sin, according to her community. "Sometimes it feels like a dream. Like I'm going to wake up one day on the compound with a baby nursing at my breast and a husband fucking me from behind at the same time."

I cringe. "The imagery, Daisy. Please."

A sad smile. "It's an actual story from my oldest sister. Gemima came to tell my father, to ask him to make her husband stop. My father told her she was a bad wife and mother. She left crying. I was only eight years old at the time, eavesdropping from the door."

We grow quiet as the bartender delivers our drinks. Gone are the playful winks from before. At least he can read the room. He gives us a solemn, almost understanding nod, even though there's no way he could have overheard us.

I ordered the Midsummer Night's Dream cocktail mostly because I've always loved the fairy Robin Goodfellow and dreamed of having her powers. And because I love cold lemonade. The menu lists fresh squeezed lemons, honey, cherry tea, smashed blackberry, and vodka.

I'm hoping it tastes good, of course.

But I don't expect it to look so freaking gorgeous.

Striated colors create a summer sunset: deep blue on top of purple, which rests above a layer of deep red. The bottom contains the last vestiges of sunlight, a pale peachy yellow. An impossibly slender slice of a lemon has been twisted around a toothpick, along with half a blackberry, and green mint leaves.

My eyes widen as I take a sip. Tart. Sweet.

And a faint burn that I know to hold my breath as I swallow.

I remember Professor Stratford telling me that oxygen makes it burn. Remember his dark eyes in the dim bar light, remember his low voice. Remember every second of what we did in the hotel room after. God, I shouldn't be thinking of him. Not here. Not when I'm surrounded by random guys who *aren't* professors. Not when I might actually belong somewhere.

"I've never met him, but I don't like your dad."

"Same with your dad," she says, lifting her glass of water.

I clink before taking another long swallow. It's really delicious. The bartender can make drinks like this? It's so much better than the alcohol at the hotel. "So what happened?"

"He's always been softer with me, you know. More lenient." Daisy grins, briefly, revealing such an infectious exuberance that it's immediately clear why her father occasionally bent for her. "He let me finish high school. I applied to Tangle-wood in secret. He about lost his shit when I told him, but in the end he let me come."

"You're a grown-up," I say quietly.

"That doesn't really matter in our communi-ty. Women still serve men."

I know that but... "You got out."

"Did I?" She offers a vague smile. "The church leaders have been wearing him down. They never stop talking about how I'm going to hell—and that I'll take the rest of them with me, somehow. That it's his job to save me. He told me today that I had to stop. That I would get married. He already had the person picked out."

The horror makes my throat close. There's so

much to unpack. So I fight it, but in the end I ask an inane question. "Who?"

Her beautiful face is expressionless. "My uncle."

I spew a mouthful of alcoholic lemonade onto the bar top. "Holy shit."

"Holy indeed," she agrees.

"Is that even legal?"

A half-hearted shrug. "It's happened before. Not a lot, but in this case, since I'm such a difficult case, they wanted me with someone who could control me."

"Absolutely not. No. I will literally fight them."

"We argued. I thought… I thought there was a chance he might not let me leave."

A knot forms in my throat. "Like hold you prisoner?"

Her blue eyes turn dark with sadness like the purple blue of my drink, like the dome of a warm midsummer night. "In the end I was able to leave, but I'm not sure I can go back. I think they'll be…ready. I think they're preparing for it right now. Planning."

"Then you absolutely cannot go back." I would actually fight for her. If she didn't come back, I would go to where she lived and try to get her out…but with what resources? I'm just one girl without any resources. And I'm not sure the police would help. Especially if the group has managed to sustain their practices for so many decades.

"And never see my sisters again? Never see my nieces and nephews?"

My heart clenches. "I'm so sorry."

"Hey, at least I have experience fucking old guys that I don't actually like. Maybe college really did prepare me for my adult career as a fundamentalist wife."

"I thought… At the hotel you seemed so cool about it, I thought you didn't mind."

"I don't. Not really. Not any more than I mind praying and repenting and churning actual butter back home. They're both just parts I play. Roles, like in those plays you like. The real Daisy Bradshaw? I don't think I'll ever meet her. I'm not sure she even exists."

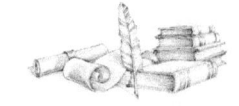

CHAPTER FIFTEEN

Interesting Specimen

I TAKE HER hand beneath the bar top, the one closest to me, and squeeze in private solace. We're in the middle of a room full of people who are drunk and dancing and shouting. For a moment it's just the two of us in a small bubble of shared understanding.

The bartender returns with a dark red martini with black salt around the edge. He slides it to Daisy. "A Bloody Macbeth," he announces. "From the gentleman at the end."

We both look over where a man stands, his blond hair thick in the glittering light, his eyes mischievous behind the mask. He wears a white T-shirt, black suit jacket, and skinny jeans. He nods to us, and I recognize him as Tyler from my literature class.

"Wow," I murmur. "He cleans up nice."

"You know him?" Daisy asks, sounding grateful for the distraction.

The bar is thick with people chatting and others waiting to order drinks. Tyler makes his way through them, a glint in his eyes. He grins at me. "Anne. Introduce me to your friend."

"Daisy, this is Tyler. Tyler, Daisy."

Daisy gives him a wave with fluttering fingertips. "Hiii."

He grins at her. "Nice to meet you. You're far too beautiful to be drinking water."

Despite my own confusion at the logic, Daisy seems to like it.

"A Bloody Macbeth," she muses, her posture shifting from defeated to flirtation in a matter of seconds. "An interesting, if eccentric, selection. What's it made from?"

He widens his eyes in mock confusion. "Why the blood of your enemies, of course."

"Oh good," she says, taking a sip while maintaining eye contact with him. "I thought it would be something boring like blackberry or grenadine."

"Never boring," he says. "That's the ultimate sin."

She laughs, and I excuse myself to go to the bathroom.

I don't really need to go, but I'm only going to be a third wheel if I stay when she's flirting. She probably needs the distraction. And the reminder that she still gets to choose her partners, that she controls her body and her future, regardless of what her father wants.

I wander into the room with poker and blackjack.

There's someone set up as a cashier. People exchange stacks of cash for little trays of chips. I wonder if there's a charity-case discount on this. I watch someone lose what appears to be a few thousand dollars before shaking my head.

Nope, my pile of cash is in my dorm room.

I wouldn't risk it on a random draw of the cards.

Maybe I should find my own random guy to flirt with, find my own temporary amnesia. Unfortunately, they all seem so…small. The kind of skinny that comes from youth. The kind of grins that come from ignorance. My heart yearns for someone older, wiser.

That's not precisely true. There are men with larger builds, even with gray at their temples. I'm not sure whether they're adult students, alumni, or even faculty.

I don't want any man. I want one in particular. One I definitely can't have.

The next room appears to be another bar, this one with darker lighting, moody music, and a more casual vibe. Sweet smoke scents the air. People lounge on sofas, some of them draped over each other. They remind me of a pack of lions lounging after the hunt, sated.

I continue down the hall.

There's one last door at the end, red light emanating from inside.

Maybe the vodka has gone to my head, but it feels trippy. Like one of those old-school film projectors that moves from slide to slide, sepia-toned memories, but instead of a happy child-hood, they're wealthy college students experiencing every pleasure known to man.

Perhaps some part of me knows before I step into the room.

The moans and gasps must escape, even over the thumping bass.

Sex.

That's what's happening in this room. People writhe on beds of padded black leather, as if the teddy bear Corduroy grew up and read *Fifty Shades of Grey*. There are chaise lounges and armchairs, all of them full of beautiful bodies in the throes of passion. Some of them have their masks on, but most of them have removed their clothes. A few red-soled high heels or black G-string panties add contrast to the movement.

Leave. That's the first thought in my mind.

I don't belong here.

Actually I'm not sure there's a place where I do belong. Certainly not my flea-ridden home. Not as the third wife of a man in a religious community. Tanglewood University has been the only place where I've even remotely fit in, but I'm constantly reminded that I'm different from everyone else. Their toned, tanned, and tattooed bodies are proof of that.

God, Professor Stratford had a tattoo. I remember it from the hotel. I never got to read the words in cursive, but they're probably some quote from Shakespeare.

Even he would fit in here, with his hard muscles and commanding sexuality.

Meanwhile I'm a pale, awkward idiot who doesn't belong anywhere.

They don't discuss Shakespeare, Daisy said. *They live it.*

There must be a hundred hearts falling in love and breaking here tonight.

Betrayals. Feuds. Ascendancies to thrones—the business kind, though actual royal titles are possible at Tanglewood University. Barons or dukes or even a prince.

They're living Shakespeare, and like always, I'm turning the pages, reading along, studying them, separate. Despite my hope of fitting in here, I'm still an outsider.

A murmured voice comes from behind me. "Enjoying yourself?"

Electricity runs through my body, lighting up every nerve ending, making my nipples hard. It could be anybody with that voice, anyone with a low masculine drawl. I shouldn't recognize the timbre. Shouldn't hear it in my dreams. My body doesn't know whether to imagine him telling me that my breasts are "a perfect handful" or whether to have him lecture about idioms in the Tudor period. Both, really. Both of them make me hot.

What the hell is he doing here?

It's as if my desires conjured him. Because there's no way a *professor* should be at a super secret society's masquerade ball. Even though some people here seem older, that's very different from being authority figures on campus.

Am I enjoying myself, feeling so apart, so separate?

"Yes," I say, turning to face him, lying with my chin raised.

He's startling in his black domino mask and tailored black suit. A black embroidered vest provides texture to the sleek ensemble. It's different from the tweed jacket and white button-down he wore to class. Different from the tux he wore at the hotel.

"Really?" he asks, doubt effervescent in his voice. "What do you like best? That man there, fucking her mouth while she's upside down on the bed? Or that throuple, him fucking her from behind while she sucks his brother?"

"His…brother?" She's having sex with two brothers?

I gave Professor Stratford a hard time for *old-fashioned patriarchal bullshit* the first time we met, but I'm the one scandalized. I'm a Regency maiden seeing marble statues for the first time. Except these are very, very alive.

"How do you know?"

"Or perhaps," he says, without answering, without touching me somehow moving me, the heat and force of his command alone turning me to face the deepest corners of the room, "perhaps you enjoy that woman strapped down to a bench, a dildo inside her pussy and ass, while a line of men wait their turn for her tongue?"

A deep sensual shake begins inside me. I'm

scandalized, yes, but I'm also turned on. I don't know whether it's what I'm watching.

Or whether it's Will's low voice describing it.

"Yes," I manage, gasping out the words.

I don't know where this truth is coming from or why. A masquerade party isn't the place for honesty. Or maybe it's the perfect place. Maybe the masks give us courage we'd never have without them. Maybe he's part of a fever dream induced by something they put in that drink.

"I want you to touch me."

He groans, low and long, pressing his front to my back. "What's your name?"

He doesn't recognize me? For a moment there's a pang of hurt. Am I so forgettable that even after the hotel, even after his office, he doesn't know me? Then I spy the glint of mischief in his dark eyes, through the mask. The hint of a smile playing at the corner of his lips.

He knows exactly who I am. He also knows that our identities would put a stop to this forbidden encounter. And I *want* this. I want one more night with him.

"We're just two people having a good time. Anonymous."

"Anonymous," he says, slowly, as if tasting the word.

A firm hand presses against my stomach and pulls me back. The pressure gives me the hard, long shape of his cock.

"So I can do anything I want, any dirty, rough, indecent thing. And you can enjoy it, can't you? You can enjoy it without reservation because we're strangers."

I nod, unable to speak around the thick knot in my throat. That's exactly what I want. What I need. How does he know that? Even when he's doing filthy, humiliating things to me, he seems to know it's what my body desires—even before I do.

"Come on, then." He links his hand to mine and leads me into the hallway. I'm not sure what I expect. This is the sex room, and we're going to have sex, aren't we? Is there another one? I wouldn't put it past them. But when he presses through the door at the end of the hallway, the one almost invisible because it's the same black as the walls, we're somewhere else.

In a long gray corridor, dimly lit from triangular metal lights above.

"Why are we leaving?" I whisper.

He glances back, though whether in reassurance or warning is unclear. "I'm taking you where no one can see you come for me. Those boys don't deserve your body."

The door behind us closes with a hard, metallic latch. The music and moans evaporate into a distant ringing in my ears. We're alone in this underground tunnel with no one else.

He could do anything to me here.

I come to a halt, pulling my hand from his. "What is this place?"

"A connection between buildings."

"Between bomb shelters?"

"Something like that," he murmurs.

"Do you know where it leads?"

"There's no part of this school I don't know."

The certainty of his words makes me shiver. As does the broad line of his shoulders as he leads me down the hallway.

Our footsteps echo on concrete.

A door leads us to a similar basement, this one empty.

My eyes widen behind the mask. This was...what? Some kind of bomb shelter? One corner holds a small pile of dusty boxes and one of those old fat monitors from decades ago. "Why doesn't the university use this place? They always need more space."

"The administration doesn't know it's here."

"What?"

"The records have been erased. The locks changed."

"By the Shakespeare Society? How would they get that kind of power?"

He leads me up a stairway. "That's the thing about power. It's not handed out. It's taken."

His voice echoes almost ominously in the empty space. We end up in the darkened, wood-paneled hallway of a building I don't recognize. Doors to classrooms line the walls, the windows half-covered with broken blinds.

"Are you going to teach me something?" I ask, not sure where the taunt comes from.

He turns back, a small smile playing on his lips. "Do you want to learn?"

"It depends on what you know."

"I think," he muses, his voice low and dangerous, "what I'd most like to teach you is a lesson. A lesson not to go into private rooms or dark hallways with strange men. Anything could happen to you. Anything at all."

I shiver at the threat, even though I know he wouldn't hurt me.

I know *him*.

That's how I find myself stepping inside a classroom style that feels quite old. There are steps on the side that lead to slightly elevated rows of seats. The front has a plain, large wooden table—no desk or podium or projector here.

Just a green chalkboard with broken white pieces on the metal sill.

Something has been left written there, some series of numbers and angles. It feels like my trigonometry class from high school, only far more advanced. Daisy probably knows what it means.

Professor Stratford erases the lines and symbols as best he can, the old chalkboard resisting his efforts. When there's only a green-white cloud, he finds a piece of chalk. That familiar block handwriting appears...

1) *Take off the dress*
2) *Leave the mask on*
3) *Bend over the table*

My intense drive to be a good student collides with my secret sexual desires. It leaves me breathless. He turns to face me. Even with the mask, I can see his expression of stern expectation. *I'm waiting*, the set of those broad shoulders say.

I push thin straps down my shoulders and let the slinky material fall to the floor.

He doesn't move, not even a muscle. He might be watching a student recite an oral presentation for all the interest he shows. Except for the impressive bulge in his pants. That makes it clear that he's far from unaffected. Daisy's strapless bra didn't fit me, so I chose not to wear anything underneath. My breasts are free, bare to the desks and chairs and chalkboard, bare to the high, thin windows that probably look out over campus. Exposed.

Except for my thin black panties.

They only seem to emphasize my nakedness, though.

The chalkboard said nothing about panties, only the dress. Being the good, obedient student that I am, I leave them on. And bend over the table, my hands flat on the surface, fingers spread wide. Goose bumps rise over my skin. Not because I'm cold. Not because I'm afraid. Because desire rushes through me like thick honey, so sweet it aches at the back of my throat.

I'm facing the front of the classroom, able to see the chalkboard and those blocky, dominating words if I look up. He steps behind me, and I feel nothing but empty air.

"Welcome to class," he says, and I startle.

His hand lands on the side of my hip, calming me, settling me as if I'm an animal.

"Here we have an interesting specimen to

study," he continues. "A woman in her most intimate place. This one's aroused. I think she likes being on display."

A desperate moan escapes me.

He chuckles. "Yes, she does. You'll find that about some women. They like being displayed. They like being touched and licked and fucked in front of people. It's a good thing we have such a fine selection for our demonstration."

His hand runs over my ass.

"Smooth." His voice is cool, distant observation, loud enough to reach the back of the class, those empty desks watching, watching. He runs a hand into the crease, touching a finger to the puckered entry. I gasp in shock. "And here, very tight. Very sensitive. You don't want to practice insertion here unless your subject has been adequately prepared."

My eyes widen. Is he talking about anal sex?

I'm definitely not properly prepared.

My ass tenses.

"No," he says with a firm, sharp slap on my butt cheek. I cry out in surprise more than pain. His shoe nudges my right leg to the right. Then my left leg to the left. I'm more exposed than ever. "Specimen responds well to correction, as you can see. It even makes her more wet." His finger trails down, down. Into the tender folds of my flesh.

I already know I'm wet, can already feel the slick slide.

"The good news," he says, "is that they seem to enjoy it. And it makes these gorgeous pink marks. A true marvel of nature, don't you agree? Now let's see what else we can observe."

Two fingers press through my center and then surround my clit.

I squirm. "Oh God."

"Deep inside the petals you can find a particular place, a particular knot of nerves that becomes hard and swollen with manual stimulation." As if to demonstrate, he rubs those two fingers in circles.

"Please," I say, trying to press up onto my toes. The high heels don't let me move much. My sex clenches, and a single heavy drop of arousal falls inches down the inside of my thigh. The words almost spring from my lips: *Please, Professor Stratford.*

Except I don't want this to end—the anonymity. I need it.

"There are several ways to manipulate this bundle. With my fingers, as you can see here. With the palm of my hand for a more blunt approach." He presses hard, and my eyes roll back. "You can also reach the back of it through the specimen's channel." Two fingers push inside me, searching, reaching for a particular place. When he finds it my knees collapse. I would fall down if his hand wasn't there to catch me around the waist. He sets me gently on the table, my breast and stomach pressing against cool wood. I'm fully a specimen now. Fully his.

"And then there's my favorite way. I could describe it, but I'd rather show you."

I shiver, not sure what to expect. Not even when I feel him move behind me, move and lower. Large hands prop my ass higher on the table, revealing me fully. His warm breath caresses sensitive skin coated in my own arousal.

It feels unbearable. Unbearable and so, so good.

He licks me with calm command. Even without his words, his tongue busy at work, his face pressed between my legs from behind, it feels like he's demonstrating something for a large class. The idea of a room full of frat boys watching him makes me groan. They would all be hard, all want to fuck me, but they wouldn't know how.

Professor Stratford shows them what to do, teaches them with every lick, every stroke of his fingers on my clit, his other hand holding my hips steady, how to pleasure a specimen such as me. "Tell them." The words are almost a snarl. "Tell them how it feels."

"So good," I cry. "It feels so good. I can't stand it. I never want him to stop."

"Good girl." He rewards me for my answer by licking me again, biting gently.

A high-pitched sound escapes me. "No one ever... No one's ever made me feel like this. I didn't even know... Didn't know my body could do this. Didn't know I needed you." Pleasure looms over me, the shadow of an impossibly large wave. I'm going to drown. "Please," I beg, unable to stop myself. "Please, please. Please make me come, sir."

The last word comes out without any decision. It's from that night.

From the hotel room.

It's also something we can call men in authority, something we can call professors.

I might have been saved, might have survived it, except that he twists those fingers back inside me, finding the space that makes my head toss back, that makes my mouth open on an empty scream. He bites into the flesh of my ass cheek, the same place still tingling from where he slapped it. The hint of pain sends me over, into the deep space of eternal climax.

"Professor Stratford," I cry, pleasure striking me again and again, almost too acute. I need it to stop, but I also don't want it to end. "Please. *Will.*"

Ripples of pleasure continue for what feels like forever.

I might have lain on this desk for hours or even days.

He turns me over gently, allowing me to rest on my back as I catch my breath and float down to earth. His hands stroke over my body, intimate but not sexual, calming me. When I open my eyes, there's glitter caught in the web of my lashes, the mask askew.

"Oh God," I whisper, as it fully hits me that I'm naked in the middle of a classroom. Then I realize he's still hard. He didn't have an orgasm. "You need...something. I have to..."

"You did so well," he murmurs, with a long stroke from the base of my neck, through the valley of my breasts to my belly button. "Took it like such a good girl for me."

Even exhausted and sated, my pussy clenches at his words. "Professor..."

"It's okay, dear heart. I know what you needed."

Of course he knew. It's a dark magic he has.

I was aroused by the public sex in the masquerade, but I also didn't want to be seen. I felt separate, but maybe I also needed the separation. He knew that, the same way he understood instinctively that I needed the fake anonymity.

The masks were just a pretense, after all.

A way to pretend along with the hundred imaginary people in the seats.

A game that we play to cover up the fact that we shouldn't be together.

That we know it will lead to tragedy. That the man gently lifting me like a doll, pulling the dress over my arms, can never really be mine.

I don't belong with him.

I don't belong anywhere, and I pull away from him in a rush.

"Anne," he says. "You're distressed. Wait."

"Wait for what?" Panic rises in my throat. Or maybe that's hysteria. I push away from him. "You're my *professor*. What are you even doing at this masquerade?"

He sighs. "It's complicated."

"Let me uncomplicate it. What happened between us was two masked strangers."

"You knew who I was, dear heart." His voice

is gentle, which makes it worse.

An uneven laugh escapes. "I know a lot of things, like the fact that you shouldn't be with me. And I can't be with you. I know that and somehow I keep ending up here, naked and wet and stupid. So damn stupid even though I know better."

I turn and run back through the long hallway, half hoping he'll follow me, half dreading it. But I reach the masquerade party without being stopped, passing the sex room without seeing, my eyes blurred with a veil of unshed tears. I refuse to let them fall.

I find Daisy in the gambling room with Tyler. She's laughing as the table applauds her.

Apparently she's won.

She should stay here and have fun.

Too late. She sees me. Her hands grasp my arms. "Annie? What's wrong?"

I can't answer her.

It's a secret. Like this masquerade party, only more dangerous.

I think it's breaking my heart.

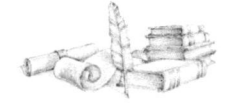

CHAPTER SIXTEEN

Tanglewood Tea

MY EYES FEEL gritty when I open them, as if I slept facedown on a beach instead of a couch in someone's private dorm room. Which I did. I drag myself back to my dorm, slipping past other students who look bright-eyed as they head toward class. All the hot water is gone this late in the morning, so I take a brisk shower and throw on clothes.

I'm fifteen minutes late when I arrive at the building, a first in my college career.

Class discussion already bustles along as I slip inside and grab a seat.

They're reading from the infamous balcony scene.

What's Montague? It is nor hand, nor foot,
Nor arm, nor face, nor any other part
Belonging to a man. O, be some other name!

I can't help but see the parallel between being a Montague and being a professor. I know that he's forbidden to me. I can't fraternize with a teacher. And he can't be with me.

But when we're together it doesn't feel forbidden.

It feels right.

He isn't Professor Stratford in those moments.

He's simply a man.

A handsome, brooding, dominant man who makes my body sing.

The person beside me has their phone up, which is rare in this class, but I peek over and see the logo for Tanglewood Tea. *Orgy at the Masquerade Ball.* Oh God. My stomach clenches around a giant rock. That's not exactly keeping things under wraps.

It makes me wonder why Professor Stratford was even there.

How did he know about it? Did someone tip him off under pain of death?

No, because most professors would have alerted the authorities.

Did he know I would be there? Did he guess?

Was he looking for me?

The siren call of that makes me shiver. I shouldn't want him to be looking for me.

Because it's dangerous. For him. What if the Tanglewood Tea had caught a photo of him? The headline would read a lot differently if they had. And it's dangerous for me. Because if they had caught that photo, I would have been exposed— in every way.

> *Romeo, doff thy name,*
> *And for that name, which is no part of thee,*
> *Take all myself.*

Professor Stratford holds up his hand to signal a pause to the reading. "And so Juliet declares that he can have her, as long as he renounces his identity. Quite a choice."

Someone snickers about being pussy-whipped.

Another laughs, claiming that they've never had pussy if they aren't whipped.

Someone raises their hand.

Professor Stratford nods to them.

"Professor, can you tell us about the Shakespeare Society?"

I go still. The entire room stills. No one's tapping a pen or scrolling on their phone right now. At this precise moment, he has more control over the classroom than any other professor on campus. I shiver at the memory of his hand slapping my ass.

He cocks his head. "Despite the name, I'm not sure it's particularly on topic."

"Of course it is," they argue. "You've been telling us that themes of Shakespeare never die. What could be more relevant than a group of students parading around as his disciples?"

That earns them a faint smile. "Fair enough. What do you want to know?"

"Where did it start?"

He takes his time answering, moving behind the podium for the first time. Perhaps he wants the distance between the class as he discusses something so close to us. Or perhaps he's thinking of what we did last night, hard beneath his dark slacks. Perhaps he's thinking of showing the entire classroom, not empty, but *this* class, how to make me come.

My cheeks flush at the possibility.

"How long has Tanglewood University had female students?" he asks.

There's a pause while we take in the apparent change in direction.

An image comes to mind of a mural painted across the wall in the bursar's office. It has a history of the university, from its founding in the 1800s to the present. Notable moments are pulled out with photos and explanations, including the creation of major landmarks and monuments on campus and notable minds making history who graduated from here. These include Nobel laureates, politicians, actors, activists, and C-level executives in the Fortune 100.

There had been an entry for when women were allowed admission.

"Nineteen seventy-one?" It comes out as a question, my voice lilting up.

Professor Stratford looks at me with approval in his dark eyes. There's knowledge in that darkness, knowledge of both sex and foolish dreams, of both my body and my mind.

He nods. "There was a lot of social pressure to allow women in by that time. There are also some embarrassing remarks from deans and administrators who fought against the change. Which should be proof enough for you all to question everything we say."

A few students chuckle.

"However," Professor Stratford says, his voice thoughtful. "There was at least one female student before that. Back in eighteen eighty-four. She applied using her initials. Admissions assumed she was a man, and with her stellar accomplishments, naturally accepted her."

"Cross-dressing," someone says with a loud,

fake cough.

"Ah," Professor Stratford says. "That would probably have happened if this were a Shakespeare play. Indeed, there may have been even more female students who did that and were never caught. This particular student, Florence Elizabeth Hart, or F.E. Hart, according to her official transcript, didn't hide her gender."

He pauses, letting us imagine it.

A strong hand sweeps across his body. "There was an uproar. Professors refused to teach her. Donors threatened to pull support. The administration attempted to remove her, but there were no grounds. So the board voted unanimously to bar women from entry so that no one could follow her footsteps. But Hart was allowed to stay. She studied here, received top marks in all her classes, but was denied a diploma at the end."

"Fuck," someone says.

"Yes," Professor Stratford agrees. "The Shakespeare Society was founded in rebellion to that action. Its aim was to make Shakespeare accessible to all people—regardless of gender, race, or class. There were plays performed in secret, readings."

"Truth to power," someone says, kicking off a round of commentary.

"Who knew Shakespeare could be cool?"

another says.

"Shakespeare Revolution," a boy shouts, creating laughter.

I raise my hand and continue as he nods. "Was anyone ever hurt?"

The room quiets.

"Like many movements," Stratford says, "there was a charismatic founder who led the charge. He mobilized people with his own passion for the mission. And he had a girlfriend who had graduated valedictorian of her high school class, but who was denied entry to Tanglewood under the new bylaw. Together, they determined to give her the education she deserved."

The education she deserved.

It's an interesting idea.

Do I deserve an education? I've fought for it, but it's never been a sure thing.

"And like many movements, there were detractors. The school itself was determined to put an end to such a thing. They considered teaching women blasphemous, an affront to the men who would be true leaders and thinkers. This kind of thinking from the administration itself encouraged angry, violent, scared students to fear the society. To seek it out. To try and ferret out its members. It was an era of academic McCarthyism."

Someone from the back speaks. "People complain about statues of southern Civil War generals being taken down. It's history, they say, even if it's ugly. But isn't this history?"

"That's right," he says. "All history is revisionist history. There's always someone telling the story. And the university would rather people not look too deeply at that time. It detracts from their status as a producer of great thinkers to show that its students, as well as its faculty, were so prejudiced and bitter...and violent."

You could hear a pin drop in the large lecture hall as he pauses.

"Were they caught?" Tyler asks, looking worried.

A short nod. "The secret location of their meeting was leaked. And instead of being handed over to the university, it was given to the Tanglewood City Police under the claim that they were fomenting insurrection against the government. There was a raid."

Oh God.

"The students at least had a reason to be on campus, but the girlfriend, she didn't. Her boyfriend refused to leave her, even when the armed men demanded it. Especially then. He didn't trust them with her. And so they shot him. And when she lunged at them in fury over his death, they killed her, too."

Goose bumps rise on my skin.

Professor Stratford looks down, and I have the most terrible sensation. Emotion moves through him. Without even seeing his dark eyes, with barely a shudder of his large frame, I can see it. I think everyone can. He picks up the book with its worn, yellowing pages. "That's why we learn Shakespeare," he says, his voice low and rough. "Not because he was a genius wordsmith and poet. Not because he changed the landscape of literature. Those things are nice, but the reason we study his works is because they never stop being relevant. They're not about counts and kings and witches. They're about humans. They're about us."

His eyes meet mine on that last sentence. *They're about us.*

My breath catches.

Only then do I realize that my face is hot with emotion. That my heart pounds with awareness. The yards between us, the desks and podium, evaporate into nothing. I want him, despite the rules, despite everything, and in this moment, I know he wants me back.

That he's fighting the same losing battle.

His passion drenches the entire room—with sadness, with pain.

And with a determined hope that makes me realize why someone would bother patiently explaining the meaning of obscure words like *amerce* and *caitiff* and *ropery* to a bunch of tired, hungover teenagers.

"After the bloodshed in the raid, there was backlash. Students and faculty alike held protests and circulated pamphlets. New bylaws were created to establish the right of students to form groups and gather on campus safely. But the Shakespeare Society, what was left of it, was understandably fearful. They reacted with ever greater secrecy. And without their leader to guide them, in the decades that followed the mission became...fractured. There were parties. Pranks. Stunts that were so dangerous that the university was forced into the uncomfortable position of shutting them down once again, though this time with much more circumspection."

This story is a far cry from the proud, carefully curated mural on the wall of the bursar's office. Revisionist history, indeed. I suppose it makes sense that they wouldn't want to highlight the university's darker moments during tours and registration. But without this information, how will we have the foresight to keep it from happening again?

Already there's discord when it comes to politics. We choose our sides and declare the other side cruel, or even worse in academia, stupid. There's a shutdown of communication. Of understanding. An increase in fear...and now we know. Now we know where it can lead. To two people dying in a tomb. To two lovers being gunned down over Shakespeare.

Professor Stratford stands and writes on the dry-erase board for the first time this semester. His handwriting is blocky and unapologetic.

Comparative Literary Analysis Essay
6–8 pages single-spaced, 12 pt Times New Roman
Use a minimum of two scholarly sources

As he writes, I scribble the requirements down furiously. Other students rush to grab their notebooks and laptops from their bags where they'd resided during the readings.

Even before the noise quiets down, Professor Stratford turns to face us. "Choose a tragedy from either a piece of modern media or real-life history. Compare it to *Romeo and Juliet*, with a particular focus on the opposition of aesthetics and historicism. This assignment will count for half of your grade."

A collective groan drowns him out for a brief second.

A smile flickers across his face. He sets down the marker with a definitive click. "The other half? Participation. Thank you to all who have read for us. As well as asked questions and contributed thoughts to our discussions. If you haven't, start."

Then he enters his office, shutting the door quietly behind him.

The room erupts into lively conversation about the essay, both its possibilities and the rather intense fact that it's worth so much of our grade. Plus the little surprise that our participation has been counting all this time.

"Umm, hello. A little warning? He could have told us."

"I actually knew about the whole Shakespeare Society thing," someone says, their tone rather self-important. "But now that he told everyone, I can't use it in my essay."

A long groan. "I have a major project in Greek Classics due the same week."

Worry beats in my own chest. Our assignments have usually been narrower. In our freshman analysis class, we wrote about how to use formalism to describe a specific text...after having used formalism in class to describe that very same text. It was akin to recitation. Change the words around. Make it sound like your own. Done.

This is...harder.

It's also far more interesting.

My lips quirk as I look down at my paper, notes scrawled in more of a sloping sideways cursive. He could have told us this on the first day, handed out a syllabus like everyone else. It would have meant something completely different then, without having heard *Romeo and Juliet* spoken aloud for two weeks. Without hearing the analysis, the *real* analysis, even if they came sometimes in the form of dirty jokes or snarky comments.

No, I could see the reason he'd done it that way.

Foresight isn't always a gift.

CHAPTER SEVENTEEN

Daddy Issues

B USES CIRCLE THE campus regularly. It's not always faster than walking straight across, not with waiting at the stop and the ever-present heavy traffic, but it's definitely easier.

I lean back in the plastic bucket seat and close my eyes.

Brakes squeal as the bus comes to a stop.

Brandon hops on, sees me, and freezes.

My eyes widen.

For a moment I think he's going to slide into the seat next to me. Then he hangs his head, eyes downcast, and keeps walking past me. His shoulders slump in something like dejection.

Awkward.

But also a relief? I shouldn't feel so nervous, as if I have a big scarlet letter sewn into my sweatshirt. A neon sign that says, *I had sex with your dad.*

I lean back as the bus moves again.

Maybe if we had just dated, I could have pretended not to see him.

But after the scene in the hallway, after knowing what his father feels like inside me, I'm drawn to him despite myself. He's a connection to the man who's been consuming my dreams. Maybe my only connection, my only way to learn more about him.

There are a few other people here, a young woman with a black case shaped like a violin and a couple of guys arguing about the prisoner's dilemma. Someone of indeterminate gender lies down across the bench at the very back, and I have the suspicion that they've gone a couple laps around the university.

Brandon sits on an aisle seat, and I slip into the seat across from him.

"Hey," I say.

"Hey," he says, sounding wary.

It makes me feel strange, like I'm someone to be wary of. Someone with power. Which is laughable, really. "Heading to class?"

"Yeah, Applied Technical Statistics is kicking my ass."

I wince. "That sounds rough."

He shrugs. "Yeah, well, I've got the vault."

"Right." His fraternity has class notes, and even—though this is top secret—answer keys to tests, stored in their house. It's part of the perks of being Alpha Sigma Pi. He's always been the quintessential frat boy with his messy dark-blond curls and three-hundred-dollar high-tops. It made him foreign to me, but also interesting. I wanted to know what it would be like to truly fit into this world, to never doubt your place here.

But I was always a tourist in his life.

His hands are slightly too large for his body, one resting on the seat in front of him. Those hands once touched me intimately. I know what it feels like to have his body pressing down on me, his erection throbbing, his lips insistent and slightly wet.

I also know what it feels like for his father to pull my hair, to call me a *good girl*.

My entire body flushes with shame and arousal.

He clears his throat. "Listen, I'm sorry about earlier. I know I was being an ass. No means no and enthusiastic consent and all that shit."

I blink. "Enthusiastic consent?"

He rolls his eyes. "Perks of having your dad work at your school and catching you in a private conversation. Had to deal with an entire lecture. Then I had to read a book on the 'subtle nature of true consent.'" He makes air quotes around that. "And then he made me write an essay on boundaries and respectful language."

"An essay?" My lips quirk. "Did he grade it?"

"Don't fucking laugh."

"I'm not," I say, even though I kind of am.

"The truth is that I was hurt and lashing out. Thought I could...you know...tough it out. Thought you'd rather I do that than act like a wimp pansy ass."

I'm pretty sure *wimp pansy ass* doesn't qualify as respectful language, but I suppose he has to start somewhere. And I'm strangely grateful that Professor Stratford supported me that way. It's not every father of a rich kid who would do that. Especially one who knows what I resorted to in the hotel.

A lot of men would think a woman like me doesn't deserve respect anymore.

"So your dad," I say, because it's why I came back here. To learn more about the man I should never, ever lust over. "I guess he's new to campus."

"It's so ridiculous having him here. Everyone wants me to get them an A. At least I know you don't need me for that." His expression turns hopeful. "Do you?"

"No," I say firmly, making him slump.

"Of course not. Only the guys want me to get them the As. The girls want me to get them a date. Which is disgusting. He's my father, for fuck's sake."

My cheeks feel warm. "A...date?"

"Like why are you trying to get with someone twice your age? Talk about daddy issues."

"Right," I say, my voice strangled.

Do I have daddy issues? Maybe.

I didn't exactly have a beautiful upbringing. Professor Stratford is nothing like my father, but maybe that's the point. Someone who would care about me.

Someone who would take time to teach me.

I feel like I would be attracted to Professor Stratford no matter what, but the truth is that I can't even trust myself. That's what abuse and neglect does to you. It makes you doubt your own instincts. However, even if I do have daddy issues, I'm not the only one.

Clearly, Brandon has his own.

He sighs. "It was bad enough when it was just Uncle C."

"Uncle C?"

"Oh, I guess I never told you. Probably because people get so weird about it. He's a big deal in physics or whatever. Cormac Stratford in the engineering department."

"Wait, I remember reading that name in the *Tanglewood Daily*. Something about a static electrical generator that could power wells in places with low water levels." I also remember a black-and-white photo of a severe-looking man in front of a large machine. "That's your *uncle*?"

"Yeah," he says, sounding glum. "Uncle Asher would probably be a professor, too, if he were still here."

"Oh, I'm sorry."

"No, no. He didn't die. At least, probably not." He waves the question away. "I come from a family of fucking geniuses. It's really annoying."

It sounds like a dream. A family that doesn't berate you for wanting to read. "Why?"

"Nothing I do is ever impressive or interesting. My dad was summa cum laude, editor of the *Tanglewood Daily*, Whitlow Undergraduate Fellowship. Even though my mom hates him, she never lets me forget anything he did, especially when I come home with a fucking C."

Sympathy makes me scrunch my nose. He used to talk about how much pressure his mom put on him when we were dating. Strange to think that the demanding, controlling woman Brandon described was once married to Professor Stratford.

Unless... "So, are they married?"

"Nah. Divorced a couple years ago." He sighs. "They wanted to wait until I was old enough. As if I'm an idiot. I may not be a genius, but I'm not blind. Like I couldn't see that they hated each other. They never even lived in the same house."

"Oh. So you didn't live with...with Professor Stratford?" I almost said Will, almost called him by his first name, something I would *never* do for another professor.

"Mostly he flew me out to DC for the summers or Christmas break. He hates coming to Tanglewood, but he'd still show up for my birthdays and shit. I was shocked when I found out he was moving here, even if it's only for a semester."

"If he hates it so much, why did he take the job?"

"Some kind of twisted alumni loyalty, maybe? He didn't tell me. He's usually too busy telling me what I did wrong. I can never make him happy."

"I'm sure he's proud of you," I say, even

though I don't really know. It's not like we talked about his feelings about parenting in between rounds of forbidden sex. "Maybe that's why he took the job. So he could spend more time with you."

He rolls his eyes. "Whatever."

The bus slows at my stop, held up by the heavy flow of pedestrians. They always get right of way on campus, regardless of what the crosswalk says.

"Maybe give him a chance? It's nice to have a father who cares."

He looks over at me and smiles, a real smile that makes him look kind. It was this smile that got me to go out with him that first time. "Maybe. You were good for me, Annie. Kept me humble. Reminded me that there are people who have it harder than me."

"Thanks. I guess."

He holds up his fist.

I shake my head, but I'm smiling as I fist-bump him back.

Hathaway Dormitory has its own cafeteria, but it's small and greasy. Convenient for quick meals, but nothing like the other dorms have. Good thing the scholarship meal plan lets you eat anywhere. Which means I can make the trek across campus to Mayfair Dormitory, the newest and most expensive University-owned dorm.

That's where I'm meeting my friend Carlisle. We met last year in biology class, where we were lost in a sea of science majors. We kept our heads above water together. And then stayed in touch, despite our disparate backgrounds.

I text her when I get there. *Downstairs.*

Be right there!

The lobby area has couches and tables for studying. I grab a seat and pull out my phone. Without my permission I find myself typing in Professor Stratford's name. Daisy was right when she said I shouldn't look at his books, shouldn't find out more about him.

But the curiosity is excruciating.

I find his photo on the faculty page of Tanglewood University, along with a short biography focused on his academic interests and a bibliography of his published works. I'll have to come back to those later, because right now I'm interested in something a little more personal.

It's in the archives of the internet, a very old engagement announcement for William Stratford and Arabella Baldwin. Her family is well known for philanthropic works, the article says, which I assume means *rich as hell*.

She appears in a more recent society photo at a charity event, a gorgeous woman with full lips, a slender figure, and blonde hair in a high coiffure. It's never been more obvious that Will and I could never work. This elegant creature is a match for him. Not me.

I also find information about Cormac Stratford, both his entry on the faculty pages and articles about his discoveries. My eyes widen. He won the Nobel Peace Prize. Yeah, I suppose that qualifies as *a big deal or whatever*, as Brandon said.

There are also a few articles about the third brother.

Asher Stratford is a lauded composer who wrote his first sonata at age eight. He disappeared from the spotlight two years ago. Some speculate that he might be deceased, but there is no evidence of that.

Mysterious. And kind of scary.

"Hey." Carlisle greets me with a hug and a smile. She's got her black hair in a thick braid that forms a crown on her head. "Thanks for making the trek."

"Please. For fresh sushi? Anytime."

We both laugh, even though that's not quite true. I don't come here unless I'm hanging out with her. It's not that the food isn't amazing. It's that the dorm is too...nice. The high ceilings and balconies and chandeliers are so different from my dorm.

It occurs to me for the first time that maybe they don't just put the scholarship students in the worst, most broken-down dorm because we're not paying.

Maybe they know we'll feel more comfortable there.

Carlisle Lockwood became famous at the age of eight years old, singing on social media while her mother taped her. TikTok is the new form of pageant mom, she told me once. Her mom desperately wanted her to take the record deal she was offered, but Carlisle insisted on coming to college. She learns music theory, composition, and history. I'm honestly not sure whether it's really her passion or an excuse not to sing on stages.

She's gorgeous in that slender, Aubrey Hepburn way.

She's also wealthy and popular which makes her my literal opposite.

The main reason she likes me is that I treat her like a regular person. Which was only because I didn't know any better. In freshman orientation, I was the only one who didn't recognize her from the music videos and teen award shows.

It was only later that I saw her on Tanglewood Tea.

Pop Princess Carlisle's Field Trip to Tanglewood University!

It had been accompanied by a poster from one of her only movies. *Field Trip to Paris*, it said in playful cursive with a grinning twelve-year-old girl wearing a private school uniform. In one hand she held an American flag, in the other hand, the Eiffel tower. The background featured a cute boy and a fluffy white bichon frise.

She links her arm with mine. "And how are things in the world of Shakespeare?"

"Oh, you know," I say. "Forbidden relationships, tragic endings, that kind of thing."

"Is that so?"

"You have no idea." I pat her arm as we head into the cafeteria, where students mill around the various stations. "I'm starving. I was thinking sushi, but that Persian rotisserie chicken with saffron rice is calling my name."

Her blue eyes look troubled. "You look…different."

That's what Brandon said about me that first time at the coffee shop. Maybe losing my virginity really has changed me. Or maybe it was the time in the empty classroom, with Professor Stratford announcing his fingers in my sex.

"Different how?"

"I don't know. Maybe…distracted?"

A rough laugh escapes me. That's what being obsessed with your professor will do to you. It's something I can't seem to outrun, not when I see him at every turn. Not only the man himself, but reminders of him. "This one class is driving me crazy."

"A class, huh? Is there perhaps a *guy* in said class?"

Damn. "How could you tell?"

"Because you've literally never stressed over a class. You always ace them."

"Calculus was kind of hard," I mutter.

She raises one black, perfectly shaped eyebrow. "You got an A. So who is he?"

A professor. "It doesn't matter. It's not going to work out."

"Because it's forbidden?"

"I *might* be feeling a little dramatic. Or maybe it's just my period."

She grins. "It's the eternal question."

"I'm done thinking about him. I want to hear about you. How goes the music world?"

She looks like she wants to argue with me, but in the end, she allows me to avoid the subject for now. "Oh, just celebrating the men who write sonatas as gods while locking up female pop stars for their own good. You know, the usual."

Her tone is flippant, but there's a tension in her smile that makes me wonder. After all, I hid my own problem behind a casual joke about Shakespeare. And her mother controls her music career and contracts as her manager. It reminds me that we're all fighting here, even as we smile and study and behave like good little girls. Like Juliet.

We're all fighting to control our own destinies.

Even if it ends in tragedy.

CHAPTER EIGHTEEN

Omens and Prophecies

T HE EMAIL COMES when I'm in economics class.

The professor is talking about plane tickets, the differences between economy, economy plus, business, and first class. And how airlines both add amenities to the more expensive classes...as well as add detriments to the lower classes, even when it doesn't help the airline.

For example, the different prices of plane tickets and the economic impact that the class system has on our economy. The most efficient way to load an airplane would be back to front, but they load it backward so that the people who paid more for their ticket go first.

Even though it takes longer for everyone to get off the ground.

Another example is chocolate chip cookies

served only to first class. The small oven in the front makes them fresh and hot...and sends the scent of deprivation back to economy.

She calls it systemic stratification.

I call it...my life.

Someone could bring up the Shakespeare Society as an example. It's been two weeks since the infamous masquerade ball, two weeks since it was blasted into the internet, and no one has stopped talking about it since. Yesterday's class with Professor Stratford has made the rounds, even appearing on Tanglewood Tea this morning.

However, there's not really class discussion here.

Nothing like Professor Stratford's class.

A handful of people like me are taking notes dutifully, but most everyone scrolls their phone. Or plays Stardew Valley on their laptops. I'm pretty sure the girl next to me is sleeping, drool forming a small puddle on her notebook.

Not that I blame her.

The teacher doesn't seem to notice or really care.

Her voice has a kind of white noise quality that produces sleepiness.

With a sigh, I take a peek at my phone.

There's another text from my mom. *Miss you,*

sweetie! Come home this weekend!!!

Guilt rises like bile. I used to go back every weekend at the start of my freshman year.

Slowly it turned into two weeks. Then three.

Now in my sophomore year, I dread going back.

It should get easier with the visits farther apart, but somehow it doesn't. It's like I get used to a regular, ordered, moderately clean existence.

The re-entry is more of a shock to my system every time.

Regardless of my feelings, I have duties. Responsibilities.

Like Professor Stratford.

I text back a thumbs-up and book my bus ticket using an app.

Another text arrives: *Need money for medicine :(*

Shit. My mouth goes dry thinking of the money stashed under my dorm mattress.

Should I bring it home?

Of course I should. My mother needs medicine for cancer. What kind of monster daughter wouldn't bring the money? Then again, I might need it for books or supplies or...anything, really. There's no emergency fund. No support from home.

It felt so good to have a safety net.

So…addictive.

The economics professor has moved on to stratification in housing, including the design of suburbs and apartment complexes, the way that the lower classes are herded into particular areas by the people who own the land. That way the wealthy don't have to even see the slums or have to be disturbed by the poor's condition.

It's an interesting topic. I just wish she had less of a monotone.

My eyes keep drifting closed.

A notification lights up my phone.

I expect it to be Mom confirming my visit.

Instead it's an email from the dean's office. Adrenaline rushes through my veins. They usually contact me before the beginning of the semester to confirm my class load meets the scholarship requirements, but they already did that.

It appears to have been written by one of the administrators who work there.

Dean Morris requests a meeting. Can you come by at 3 p.m. today?

My gaze flicks to the time. My class will end a few minutes before that.

I'm guessing they already looked at my schedule and knew that.

I'm also guessing the "request" isn't really optional.

I'll be there! I type, pressing send…before realizing I just exposed myself by looking at my phone during class. No matter. The important thing is they know I'm going to be there. Did I do something wrong? A few of my classes have already had papers due. What if one of them had such a terrible grade that they called the dean's office? Can I lose my scholarship before we even reach the end of the semester?

My heart beats a thousand miles per hour, but I force myself to calm down.

I force my expression blank.

No one looking at me could tell that I'm freaking out.

And no one is around to push my head between my knees if I have a panic attack.

Breathe. I hear the command in Professor Stratford's voice.

My throat feels locked. I try to remember the feel of his strong hand making circles on my back. *You can do it, sweetheart. Take a deep breath in. Let the air inside.*

I gasp in a quick, painful gulp of air. The person next to me snores.

Good girl. Another one.

I take another breath. Slowly I calm down.

When class ends, I'm the first one out of my

seat and out the door while everyone else is still gathering their stuff. I force myself to walk at a normal pace as I cross the quad, a large four-sided courtyard with a gorgeous lawn and a massive circular fountain in the middle. I pass the library, the food court with its upstairs rec center.

The dean's office is held in the nicest building in the humanities department, with painted ceilings and oversized green marble tiles. I present myself to the secretary, who sends me through. Blood races through my veins as I try to appear everything a dean would want their full-ride scholarship recipient to be: attentive, grateful, serious. An academic paragon.

I've seen Dean Morris a few times, from far away, at ceremonies and speeches.

So I'm not shocked by the scars on the side of his face.

Through the rumor mill, I know he got them in the military. He's a hero. He was also a history professor at Tanglewood University before he became the dean.

He stands and gives me a small smile. It has the appearance of a grimace since one side pulls up and the other doesn't, but his kind eyes reassure me. "Nice to see you, Ms. Hill."

"Dean Morris." I shake his hand. Professor

Stratford's voice in my head keeps me from hyperventilating, but it can't keep my fears from spilling out. "I'm so grateful to be here at Tanglewood University. Thank you so much for the continued opportunity."

He gives me a slight shake of his head. "Sit down," he says. "And there's no need for gratitude. That scholarship was not a gift. You earned it with your hard work."

"I'm sorry if I've done something wrong."

"That's not why I've called you in. At least, not precisely."

I wish that were more reassuring. "Was my essay on omens and prophecies in Cultural and Social Anthropology wrong? I can rewrite it. I knew the comparison to modern data forecasting was a risk, but—"

"Please, Ms. Hill," he says, huffing a laugh. "Allow me to tell you why I've called you in. But also email me that paper later. I want to read it. It sounds fascinating."

I sit back, chastened. "Of course, sir."

He leans back in his high-backed leather chair. "What do you know about the Shakespeare Society?"

My throat closes. Oh God. I'm going to be expelled for going to the party.

And participating in a freaking orgy.

"I've heard about it, you know," I say. "From rumors."

"And the Tanglewood Tea?"

My cheeks flush. It's hard to imagine someone as proper as Dean Morris reading the gossip account, but of course the school would know about it. It's available online to the entire world. "Yes." I swallow hard. "And the truth is that I… I went to a party they had."

"I know."

My eyes widen. "You do?"

"Don't worry. It's not against the rules of your scholarship to attend a party. Even if that party is on campus and not sanctioned by the university. We don't hold you accountable for what the society does."

Relief floods me. "Oh, thank God."

He looks curious. "If you thought it might get you in trouble, why did you confess?"

"I'm not sure," I admitted. He does have a particularly authoritative manner. I can imagine him commanding a troop of hardened soldiers. Or a battalion. I don't really know what they're called. That's not the real reason, though. "I guess I just…think honesty is the best policy. I know that might make me sound naïve or—"

"It doesn't. It makes you sound honorable."

"And if I get in trouble for something I did, then that would mean I deserve it."

"Well," he amends. "The world isn't always as fair as that. But in this case, you have nothing to worry about. The university can't condone parties on campus, especially parties that have illegal substances and gambling, but that's the responsibility of our security department. They've been apprised of the situation and will be tightening their protocols."

"That's...good."

"Anyone caught hosting the party or helping them facilitate it will be dealt with strictly."

Does that include Professor Stratford? Probably. Even if they might let a student off the hook, I can't imagine they would allow a member of their faculty to flout the rules. Why did he take the risk of going there? Why did he take the risk of having sex with me?

"I see," I say, even though I'm plunged into even more confusion.

He nods. "It may seem harsh, but it's a question of safety."

"I—I don't want anyone to get hurt."

"Good. Then you'll understand why I need to ask you this... We need someone on the inside. A student who can blend in. Someone to find out their next move, so we can stop them."

My throat tightens. Shit shit shit.

His expression is knowing. "I appreciate loyalty. I don't make this request lightly. I suppose you've heard about the way the society formed."

I swallow around a stone. "A little."

"The excesses of drugs and alcohol would be risky enough, but there's more to the society. A deep love of the dramatic that manifests in very real danger. There were multiple injuries over the years. That's why they were originally found and shut down."

"What kind of injuries?" My voice comes out as a whisper.

"Overdoses, which don't always get caught in time due to the secrecy involved. There was a notable sword fight, I presume in the interest of historical accuracy. However, they moved on to guns. Back then the administration had some inkling that the society was forming, but they didn't realize the severity until someone ended up in the emergency room. They reported the gunshot wound to the police, who traced it back to the founders."

Oh God.

"There have also been fistfights, falls, and one

that remains a mystery—someone found half-starved in the fountain in the quad. They had been missing for a week. They refused to talk about what happened."

Fear coalesces into determination.

An underground party is risky enough. Like he mentioned, there's always the risk of overdoses. But this is so much worse. Guns? Starvation?

"How can I help? I mean, I'm not *in* the society or anything."

"It's a good sign that they invited you to the party. It means they're aware of you. But they don't just let anyone join. They don't advertise their plans, for obvious reasons. The secrecy is part of the allure. We need to find out who's started the society back up."

I frown. "I want to help. But like I said, I'm not a great liar."

I'm good at keeping secrets, a byproduct of my upbringing. Even as part of me condemned myself for being "prissy," my mother's word for me not wanting to bathe in a shower growing actual green goo, as part of me believed I deserved the backhands my father gave me, I also knew that I couldn't tell anyone about it. That what was normal in my house would be considered horrifying to other people.

So I learned to keep my mouth shut.

It became second nature.

That's different from lying. I never made up stories about an idyllic childhood.

"We think your earnest nature will make you seem less threatening to them."

Earnest nature seems like a nice way of saying *awkward outcast.* "I can't just go around asking who's running the place. I'm not even sure if they'll invite me again."

"I think they will. You've shown promise as a highly intelligent student and particularly knowledgeable about Shakespeare. They like to think of themselves as a meritocracy, almost like an academic think tank operating underground in the university."

Lead forms in my stomach. How would they know what I know about Shakespeare? Unless they're in my classes. Unless they're in Professor Stratford's class in particular.

What was he doing at that party? Did he receive an anonymous invite through a friend, like me? Or is he actually part of the society?

After all, it did start after he started working here.

Then again, he's said repeatedly that he doesn't want to be here.

Why would he get involved with restarting a society in a place he wants to leave?

I don't want to think that he would be part of something that gets students hurt.

What if he is, though?

Could I be the person who gets him in trouble?

It occurs to me that I could announce his presence at that party now. That I could ruin someone's career with only a few words. Not only about his presence at the party but also the night in the hotel. There are some men who wouldn't believe a woman, but I feel from Professor Morris's warm, respectful gaze that he might.

The power doesn't make me feel good. Instead, I feel sweaty, anxious.

"If I don't spy for you, will my scholarship go away?"

He shakes his head. "I won't let that happen."

Analyzing literature helps me read between the lines. "But someone wants it to?"

"It's been suggested as a way to coerce you into helping, but I won't do that. The truth is, I don't have to. Now that you know what's at stake, you're going to help."

I swallow. He knows me pretty well, this relative stranger.

I don't know much about him besides his military career, where he was apparently decorated as a hero. I don't see any framed medallions, even though my old physical education teacher from high school kept his displayed proudly in the auditorium.

One of the only personal touches is a photo of a beautiful woman with black hair holding a chubby, giggling baby. "Is that your family?"

"My wife, Erin," he says, his eyes turning soft. It makes him seem far less threatening, even with the scars an ever-present reminder of the dark side of war. "And our daughter. She's turning two next week. My wife assures me she's on track developmentally, but I can't help thinking she's a genius when she does anything at all. It makes me insane sometimes, thinking of the dangerous world that awaits her."

Acid burns my throat. "I'm sorry."

"We can't fix everything," he murmurs, making direct eye contact that I feel down to the soles of my feet. "But we can try. We have to. Honorable people have no choice."

CHAPTER NINETEEN

Behind the Bard

THE BECKINSALE LIBRARY of Natural Science doesn't boast lion statues.

Instead a giant bronze elephant stands on a white marble pillar.

An inscription comments on the high intelligence of the animal...

The elephant's hippocampus is larger than any species, which gives them their exceptionally long memory. It's also why they suffer from psychological flashbacks, the equivalent of post-traumatic stress disorder.

I look up at the elephant's dark bronze eyes, wrapped in wrinkled skin. A few droplets of rain dot the metal, sliding down its wrinkled cheeks like tears, leaving gleaming lines.

Foresight isn't always a gift.

Apparently, a good memory isn't either.

I'm here to work on my essay, but when I should take the elevator to the second floor where classical works reside, I find myself pressing the down arrow.

That takes me to the basement, which contains a motley assortment of rarely used materials. Old original editions too rare to throw away but too unimportant to display in glass cases on podiums. There are also strangely shaped bookshelves made to hold oversized books, some with maps or recreations of engravings, along with large wood tables to lay them out.

There's a sense of absence here from a floor not usually used.

However, it's not empty.

Alyssa is lying down underneath one of the tables, a hoodie bunched up under her head, her phone propped up on her leg as she watches something on her phone. She glances over. "Hey, it's the asshole who didn't invite me to the masquerade ball."

I wince. "Sorry. I wasn't even sure if they'd let Daisy in."

She grins, sitting up. "Just messing with you. I got in anyway."

"Oh good." We aren't particularly close, but I don't want to offend her.

"What are you doing down here?"

"Looking for a particular section. What are *you* doing down here?"

"Well, I discovered this place when I had to do a report on unconventional things made out of the human body. The Catacombs and shit like that. And I found out about this book that's made out of human skin. The binding is strung with intestinal lining."

I shudder. "That's…horrifying."

"No one ever comes down here, so I use it to chill between classes. Because my roommate blows. You and Daisy are so lucky."

I manage a smile. I've heard the roommate horror stories. "I know."

"So, what's this *particular section* you're looking for?"

After a hesitation, I decide it doesn't matter if she knows. "There are some books on the history of Tanglewood University. I wanted to see if I could find out anything about the Shakespeare Society."

She perks up. "Did they invite you?"

"No, it's just… You know. Intellectual curiosity."

That makes her snort, but she follows me down the shelves to the right one.

I brush my fingertips across the spines.

The History of Tanglewood University
Passion and Prestige: A Story of Tanglewood
    University
The Fight for Peaceful Education

I thumb through the latter, finding it to be a memoir of one of the first black men to be able to attend the college, a full century before women were given that right. Elitism and prejudice come in many forms. What other people have been barred from attending?

Another thought chills me. Who is barred from attending even now?

Even as I ask the question, the answer comes to me.

The poor.

Yes, Daisy and I and a few other students have scholarships. We were at the top of our classes, both in high school and now. We beat plenty of other very qualified students. Students who, frankly, are more qualified than some whose parents were able to pay for everything.

"*The Smartest People in the Room*," Alyssa reads from one spine. "*A Tour of the Most Impressive Students at Tanglewood University.* At least we're humble."

We think of the admissions process as a meritocracy, but if that were true, then black people and women would have always been allowed. If that were true, then lack of money could never bar a qualified candidate from attending.

Pledge, says one title. *A survey of the fraternities, sororities, and other groups at Tanglewood University.* I flip to the index, which primarily consists of Greek letters. There are also groups for music, for acting, for political leanings, for community service.

At the very end, in the smallest section so far is a section titled: *Secret Societies.*

I turn to page four hundred and nine.

Some groups choose not to register with the university's regulation board, which reviews applications annually and grants access to facilities. Sometimes this is because they are not fully formed. Other times, because they wish to hide dangerous or illegal activity.

Dangerous or illegal. Like educating women, I guess.

One secret society is for seniors only.

My eyes widen. It owns an entire island where current and past members gather.

Another society does what they call *guerilla*

acts of kindness, a mixture of community service and activism that happens overnight without anyone seeing.

The Gargoyles has its members climb the buildings at night. They walk the roofs to prove their worthiness...becoming, I suppose, shadowed gargoyles in a moonlit sky. Apparently the buildings have difficulty ratings. Advanced members even do it during thunderstorms.

I shiver, imagining the slippery stone in the rain.

Most of the societies have a strict selection process for members and traditions.

A concluding paragraph ends with a warning for students not to engage in illicit behavior. There are plenty of safe, college-approved groups, it claims. Based on the thickness of the text, I have to agree. Then again, I don't know what kind of societies fail the review. What if they're not actually promoting something dangerous...simply different?

"What are you looking for?" Alyssa asks, pulling me from my reading.

"I'm not sure," I admit.

She shudders, peeking at the page I'm on. "Can you imagine walking to class and bam, there's a dead guy lying on the sidewalk with his brain cracked open like a watermelon?"

"I couldn't imagine it before, but I can now. Thanks."

A grin. "Side effect of medical school. The body is just a collection of Lincoln Logs."

"Do you think the Shakespeare Society is dangerous?"

"I don't know," she says, her expression thoughtful. "Anyone could have gotten hurt at the masquerade ball. Overdosing, getting into a fight. Fucking someone they shouldn't. Would it be the society's fault for providing the venue?"

"You're saying people are responsible for their own safety."

"If I fall down on campus, it's not like the university is footing my medical bill."

"Good point."

There's a flaw in the logic, but I can't find it at the moment. I live in a world made of flowery language and dramatic turns of phrase. I prefer fictional deaths, thank you very much.

I push the book back into place, not sure I've learned anything. "I'm heading upstairs. Shakespeare doesn't make my head hurt as much as this."

She laughs as she returns to her nest beneath the table.

It's a relief as I head to the third floor, which houses the literature section. There are countless copies of classical texts, along with endless literary analysis.

I wander around the shelves, trying to find my focus.

There are way more people on this floor, some spread out on tables with books spread, laptops open, headphones in. The study rooms have tall, thin windows to discourage inappropriate behavior, which works only sometimes.

Silence is the required sound level in the regular library, so if someone wants to talk, they have to get a study room. Someone's inside one, talking on their cellphone.

Another one holds a study group, books open, discussion flying. A piece of paper has been taped to the narrow window, announcing it as *Comp Sci 302*.

Yet another holds a group that appears to be playing a card game. Based on their shocked reactions and muted laughter, it looks like one of those games people play with shocking, dirty things. Instead of black and white cards, these look pink with flowers.

A piece of paper taped to the window says, *Romance vs The World.*

I make a note to look up what it's about later.

When I reach the Shakespeare section, I stare at the books blankly.

My mind doesn't want to focus on my essay right now.

Many of the books focus on individual plays, some annotated versions, some translated into modern-day texts, some deep-dive critiques.

Though there are more general texts sprinkled in.

> *Everyday Life in London During Shakespeare's Time*
>
> *Quoting Shakespeare Throughout the Ages*
>
> *The Intersection of God and Shakespeare*

I usually focus on the titles, but I can't help scanning the author names.

It shouldn't matter, of course. I don't need to get more drawn into fascination with my mysterious, forbidden professor. His name appears in gold embossed text on a spine. My heart thumps in surprise, even though I should have expected it. Even though I've been wanting to find his books ever since I heard he wrote them.

> *Behind the Bard: The People Shakespeare*

Knew, Loved, and Hated

My eyebrows rise.

I flip to the back cover where scholars of other Shakespearean books call the book *illuminating*, *insightful*, and *an unraveling of a mystery*.

The book is light for a research tome, the kind that provides concise analysis rather than recited history. These are Professor Stratford's words. His thoughts. Blood pulses through my veins, as if I'm on the verge of a discovery. I can hear the opening line in his voice—spoken at the front of the classroom. Or behind me as I'm bent over a table.

> *We are made up of the people around us. My favorite food is my mother's recipe for rata- touille, at once lush and rustic. I attend kite- flying festivals because my childhood friend taught me how to not only fly but also fight them, a competition he brought with him from India. My first college girlfriend re- placed my wardrobe, taking me from indie band T-shirts to collared shirts and ascots, a style I still wear to this day.*
>
> *It was actually my high school teacher who taught history, not literature, who slid me worn copies of Shakespeare's plays when I finished my work early. And so I've always*

entered the bard's world from that perspective, with a clear-eyed view of the past.

This might seem counter to what modern society tells us. We are taught to pride ourselves on individualism and self-sufficiency. And yet humans were never meant to live alone. Families. Communities. Countries. We struggle and yearn and grow together. It's inevitable that we should also impact each other. This book takes the stance that there's no shame here. That these influences are gifts, ours to leave behind or carry with us.

From Shakespeare's father to his wife, from the first director of his acting troupe to the man rumored to have ghostwritten parts of his works, Behind the Bard *explores the people who surrounded him and how they informed his work.*

My breath is coming faster by the time I'm done reading. If this were any random book, I would find it fascinating. I would dive into the pages, but right now, all I can think about is the man who wrote them.

Ratatouille and kite flying and indie bands.

They're personal, almost intimate details of his life. They give me a narrow, deep glimpse of him, like looking into someone's boudoir through a keyhole.

It only whets my appetite for more.

CHAPTER TWENTY

Little Annie Hill

IN A WAY it's a relief to escape campus and the frenzy of gossip. Everyone is talking about when the Shakespeare Society's next event will be. Campus security can be seen patrolling all over. I'm grimly aware that I'm being watched by the administration, their own little spy.

I don't really want to narc on my fellow students.

Or on Professor Stratford.

Then again, I don't want to lose my scholarship. Or stand by while people get hurt.

I close my eyes against the dilemma on the bumpy bus ride to Port Lavaca.

The rampage of cleaning works the anxiety from my muscles, leaving me like jelly. Unlike last time when I left the same day, I take a shower when I'm done. My old room is about how I left it, a few small trophies from the science fair and spelling bee line the plywood desk. It feels like standing in someone else's room. It feels like standing in a memory.

There's no masquerade ball to rush back for this time.

I'm determined to spend a little time with my mom on this visit.

So I make some popcorn in the microwave, which sputters and starts as it turns the bag in a circle. When I pour them into a bowl, most of the pieces are burnt while the rest are unpopped. I sigh and shake a little salt on top. It'll still work.

Then I climb into their bed, squished between them.

It's a little claustrophobic, the three of us in bed, especially now that I'm grown.

Rusty strains his arthritic old legs and jumps onto the bed, curling up on top of my feet.

We used to do this all the time when I was little.

The feeling is...

Safety, my mind supplies.

I remember feeling safe like this.

Now that I'm older, I know it was an illusion.

Familiar. That's what this is.

Some little-girl part of me still craves it.

I don't really like watching TV, or this dating show which seems to be based around astrology. They're paired up based on their birth charts, and then we watch the fallout. Which is usually not very peaceful.

But I like the feeling of sitting between them, of being accepted by them.

Of fitting in—at least on the outside.

"When are you going to find some nice boy and settle down?" my mom asks. "There must be plenty of good-looking boys at that school of yours."

I flush, not wanting to think about any good-looking boys. Especially when I'm consumed by a very handsome man. Wanting him. Wondering what he's hiding. Dreading having to turn him in to the dean. "I don't really have time to date."

She meets my father's eyes across from me. "A boyfriend would make me feel better. Someone to call when you're so far away from home."

My father shakes his head. "I'd rather she dates someone from home. Plenty of strapping fellows around here. Ones who aren't afraid to work. Ones who aren't sensitive poets or some shit."

"Look," I say, desperate to change the subject. "I think the Scorpio's coming back."

That distracts them. They have a lot to say about the Scorpio.

We've gotten down to the unpopped kernels when there's a loud banging on the door. I jump, spilling some greasy kernels onto the bedspread. Causing a mess when I just cleaned everything up. "Who's that?"

My father starts swearing angry words, forceful words.

I cringe. He's dangerous when he gets like this.

My mother starts crying.

"Fuck," my dad says. "They said I'd have more time. I need more time."

Dread forms a tight knot in my stomach.

"Is that your bookie? Mom told me what you did."

He slaps me, the back of his hand a hot brand against my cheek. "Don't use that tone with me, girl. You don't know what it's like providing for this family. And you don't give a shit because you're leaving."

Heat springs to my cheeks, both pain of the slap and hurt from his words.

There's more banging. Louder, louder, as if maybe someone's trying to kick the door in. And they're definitely going to succeed.

Because everything around here is made of matchsticks.

My father is standing, shaking with rage.

I don't think it's likely that he's going to answer the door. Which means that whoever is out there is going to eventually break down the door and storm inside. Then they'll have access to my mother, who's vulnerable in bed. They're going to endanger her.

She sobs, her eyes red.

I hate it here. I hate it here so much.

That doesn't stop me from doing what I've always done: facing the problems. Fixing them, when I can. I cross the small house and open the door myself, coming face to face with… Well, not with my father's bookie.

"Red?"

The former quarterback of the Port Lavaca High School wears a leather jacket with a baseball bat propped on his shoulder. "Oh hell," he says. "Little Annie Hill. I didn't want you to be here for this."

I glance back, glad my father hasn't left the room. I don't want him near that bat.

"Please," I whisper. "We don't have any money. You know my mom is sick."

He shrugs. "I got a job to do. And you know

as well as I do that your father had no business making those bets. Now give me the keys to the truck."

Shit. "How much money is it?"

He pauses a moment. Scratches the side of his face. Sighs. "Four grand."

Holy shit. Four thousand dollars? Shock thumps in my chest. The truck isn't even worth that much. How could my father have staked it? Why does he do this? "What if I just give you a few hundred dollars?" I ask. "To tide this over."

Red shakes his head. "If it was just you and me, Annie, I would do it. But I get paid to do this job. And if I don't do it, they're gonna fire me and then they're gonna send someone else after your dad. So it's the full amount, or I take the truck."

My stomach roils. It's a struggle not to up-chuck the popcorn onto his steel-toed boots. "Hold on," I say, running to my room, where my messenger bag rests against the wall. I brought it to give to my mom for medicine, but this is more urgent.

Somehow, the medicine will have to wait.

Still kneeling by my bag, I look at this thick stack in my hands.

I slept with Professor Stratford to get this

money, debased myself for it, and now just like that, it's going to be gone. That sense of security I had? Gone.

I hand it over to Red, who counts it.

He whistles. "Damn, girl. You dealing up at that fancy college of yours?"

Drugs, he means. "No," I say, too defeated to be indignant at the suggestion.

There's no such thing as morality anymore.

There's only survival.

Maybe that's all there's ever been.

He shoves the money in his back pocket. "Consider the debt paid. Keep the truck."

"Thanks," I say, my voice wry.

He backs away swinging the baseball bat in casual, almost playful circles with one hand. It doesn't look like anything that I've ever seen someone do while playing baseball. This is purely someone who uses it to hit people.

Halfway down the gravel drive, he turns back, and I tense.

"I'll give you this advice for free, little Annie Hill. You get your hands on that kind of money again? You don't come back to this house. Not ever."

"Is that a threat?"

"It's helpful advice."

"That's not helpful when my mother is sick, Red."

He shakes his head, still backing up. "You're the smartest one in this bumfuck town, but there are still things even you don't know."

"Like what?" I challenge, stepping onto the gravel.

"Like the fact that I know every doctor in the area. And more importantly, the nurses."

My blood runs cold. Has her health taken a turn for the worse? "Is she okay?"

"More than okay," he says. "Because your mother doesn't have cancer. She never has."

The words land like an atomic bomb, blowing every last thread of familial love and hope into a ball of smoke above the house. I watch as he gets smaller and smaller on the horizon.

Sunlight glints off metal as he roars away on a motorcycle.

No. He's lying. A guy wielding a baseball bat demanding gambling money isn't exactly a trusted source. I couldn't cite him as an academic resource in my essays. He's lying. Why? To cause trouble. Who the hell knows? *He's lying.* He has to be.

I drag myself back into the house. My face feels numb.

My mother's still crying. "Did he take it?"

"Fuck him," my father snarls. "He had no right."

I shake my head. My throat feels dry. "He... No. He didn't."

"What?" My mother's tears disappear almost immediately. Did she always have that ability? Have I always been blind? I gave them so much money, even while I wore thrift store clothes and struggled to pay for books at college. "Why not?"

"I gave him the money."

My father narrows his eyes. "How much?"

"All of it. Four thousand."

"How the hell did you get that much money?" He sounds accusatory. There will be no thanks, I already know that. There will be no apology for the slap that still burns like a brand on my cheek. It feels like I'm waking up for the first time, really seeing them. As if I've lived in my own little cult my entire life, made up only of three people.

I turn to my mother. "I brought it to pay for your medicine."

She waves that aside. "Oh, that can wait."

"Can it?"

"Of course." She smiles, looking a little uncertain.

I hear Brandon's voice, and Carlisle's, telling

me that I look different. I *feel* different. It's not only losing my virginity. It's maturity. It's growing up. It's knowledge, and damn does it hurt. "Do you really have cancer, Mom?"

She forms the expected expression: outrage and hurt. If I wasn't watching so carefully, I wouldn't have noticed the small flash of guilt. "How dare you ask me that, Anne Elizabeth Hill?"

Every moment plays back to me in rapid succession. The way she always insisted that I didn't need to accompany her to the doctor's office. *I don't want you to worry about me.*

"You got the diagnosis right at the beginning of freshman year. You were so mad that I had applied without telling you, that I'd accepted the scholarship. Is that why you did it?"

Tears stream down her pale face. "Anne, please."

There had been weekly texts about the experience, ones that were gut-wrenching to read. Guilt darkened every class, because I knew I was needed at home. "What about that time that I asked you about what medicine you were taking? I looked up the name, but it said you shouldn't take it during chemo. You told me you'd misspoke, but it was made up, wasn't it?"

"How dare you?" My father advances on me, his fists clenched.

My heart thuds in warning.

He's slapped me around before, but this feels more serious.

More severe.

I never felt this way with Professor Stratford, not even when he was a stranger, not even when I was alone with him in a hotel room. The world teaches us to be afraid of random men, but I've always known that the monster in my life lived at home.

CHAPTER TWENTY-ONE

Most Excellent Fancy

I'M BLESSEDLY NUMB when I reach campus. The gray skies match my mood, threatening rain. Wind rattles the trees, showering the sidewalks with early leaves.

Daisy reclines on her bed, a thick textbook on engineering propped open on her knees. "Welcome back to the land of the living," she says without looking up.

"What's the plan tonight?"

She looks over, her expression still with surprise. "Meaning what?"

"The masquerade ball. The frat party. The dangerous prank stealing some famous school artifact. What are we doing tonight?"

My roommate and best friend sits up slowly. "What happened?"

"It doesn't matter. Nothing happened."

A slow headshake. "Spill."

Grief rises inside me, but it comes out as anger. "Nothing, okay? I have a completely normal, boring, stupid life that's not worth complaining about. I'm not some poor girl raised in a cult being forced to marry her uncle and breed a bunch of incestuous cult babies."

She flinches. "Right."

Oh God. "I'm so sorry."

Her blue eyes become veiled. She's protecting herself, and who can blame her? "Don't worry about it. It's only the truth."

"Just slap me. Punch me. Pull my hair. I deserve it."

"This is getting kinky," she says with a quirk of her pink lips. "Not that I'm complaining, per se, but maybe you can tell me what's wrong."

"I just... I can't process this. Can't talk about it. I'm sorry I took it out on you."

She scrolls on her phone. "Looks like there are a couple different parties, one at a sorority, though we might run into Brandon there. One off campus. But it's Sunday. Not sure how we can sneak past Lorelei the Dragon. Maybe if we wait until *after* she does her rounds to leave?"

"No, I was being stupid. Of course I was. You're in your pajamas."

"First of all, don't act like I couldn't be presentable in like two minutes."

"Yeah, but…"

"Or that I couldn't make pajamas the next campus party trend."

I raise one eyebrow. "Doubtful."

"It's called panache, and I've got it in spades."

My heart softens. I'm grateful she forgave me. "Yeah, you do."

"So what'll it be?"

I want another distraction, another masquerade party to make me forget, another night of meaningless sex with a masked professor. Except the sex was far from meaningless. And the masquerade party only drew me in deeper. "Let's… Let's just stay in tonight. Please."

She studies me for a long moment.

I look away, but she's already seen it. She flips on the light and gasps.

"That fucker," she says, her voice cold.

A shiver takes me. "It's fine."

"It's not fine." Despite the harshness of her voice, she's gentle as she turns my chin to get a better look at the black eye that's been forming over the bus ride. "Let me get some ice."

I close my eyes, trying to ignore the cold pit in my stomach.

Except when the door opens again, it isn't Daisy.

It's Lorelei, the resident advisor. Her heavily lined eyes don't even widen when she sees my black eye. "Do I need to call the cops?" she asks, her voice surprisingly soft.

"No, thanks."

"Thank God. I hate paperwork." She tosses a piece of paper onto my bed. "Someone left this for you."

We can get mail here, but it usually comes into our cubbies downstairs. And this doesn't appear to be in an envelope or stamped. "What is this?"

"I'm not your fucking secretary," she says before closing the door.

I pick up the paper and turn it over.

It's soft underneath with words embossed into it.

Shakespeare Society, it says.

There's an image that matches the menus from the underground bar—a hand holding a skull. *Hamlet.* A moment of comedy in an otherwise tragic tale.

My heart pounds. It's happening. Dean Morris was right. In a way I thought he wasn't. Or maybe that was simply wishful thinking. If I had no information, I couldn't betray it.

Welcome, students of infinite jest, of most excellent fancy.

It's a quote from the same gravedigger scene, where Hamlet finds the skull of someone he knew. The court jester, who represents the inevitability of death, the futility of our actions. Because no matter how happy we are in life, we end the same way. It's the point of no return in Hamlet's spiritual journey, for he can no longer make sense of his existence.

A shiver runs through me.

Nihilism, then. That's the meaning of the grand parties.

The belief that nothing matters, for whether someone is good or evil, happy or sad, rich or poor, they will turn to dust in the end. So there's no reason to strive, to struggle. No reason to worry about rules or safety. No reason to give a damn.

Which, in a way, is the very opposite of what the founder intended. For his purpose was to share Shakespeare's works, to give and include under the belief that acts have meaning.

Who runs the society now? Why have they restarted it?

And how far will they go to prove their point?

It's Yorick's skull that inspires Hamlet to finally kill Claudius.

Instead he finds himself killed—a stark confirmation of the inevitability of death.

My stomach clenches.

It's shocking and worrying, but also…intriguing. Not the elitism. Not even nihilism. It's the idea that I might be part of something. That I could belong.

I need it now more than ever.

There is nothing else on the invitation. No address or time of the next meeting. Not even an email address. I flip it to the back, which is empty. The person who left this must have left this for me. Which means they're in the society.

Urgency overtakes me. Maybe I can catch them. I rush out the door and reach the end of the hall, where Lorelei's room is, the better to watch us come and go. Though her door is closed now with a sign that says, *If you need me, don't.* I press the button for the elevator and hear it rattle from the top. I push into the stairwell. There's no one inside, no sounds of steps.

Whoever left the invitation is long gone.

Back inside the room, I pace.

Daisy bursts in. "I got frozen peas from the kitchen. Don't ask me how I did it without alerting suspicion, you don't want to know. I also got some generic Advil." She holds up a bottle. "And the pièce de résistance, cheap wine."

I hold out the black card for her to read.

"Oh. My. God. Are you going to do it?"

"I don't know. There aren't any instructions or anything."

She lifts it to the light, as if the black cardstock might be see-through. "Maybe it's some kind of puzzle? Like invisible ink. Or a Bluetooth transmitter inside."

I wouldn't put either of them past a society that's so bent on secrecy.

And intellectual elitism.

But after working on the invitation all night, neither Daisy nor I can find any other clues. It appears to be ordinary cardstock that's been engraved. There's no way for me to reply to the invitation. No way for me to join the society.

CHAPTER TWENTY-TWO

Gifted Student

I HAVE ONE last idea about the invitation.

One more person who might know how to solve the riddle.

Someone who was there at the masquerade ball.

I don't even know whether I want the answer for myself or for Dean Morris, but none of it will matter if I can't figure out how to actually accept the invitation.

It's late in the day. A few students lounge on benches or spread out on the grass. The storm that has been threatening feels thick in the damp air. The coffee cart is shut down, closed up for the weekend. Sometimes the doors to buildings are locked, but the metal bar moves when I push. Then I'm in the hallway, the one where I found out that Professor Stratford is Brandon's father.

The door to the classroom *is* locked.

I slide my glance to the side. The office door is closed. At six o'clock on a Friday evening, there's no reason to think he would be here. His classes would have ended hours ago. I knock anyway. A shuffling from inside makes my chest tighten.

Then he's opening the door.

I've seen different versions of him: the wealthy gentleman at the hotel, the knowledgeable professor in class, the playful deviant at the masquerade ball. This is an entirely new version: dark hair askew from running his large hands through it, sleeves rolled up on a rumpled white button-down, an early evening shadow of scruff darkening his sharp jaw.

His dark eyes widen when he sees me.

And the bruise that makeup can't quite hide.

He pulls me inside. "Who the hell did this to you?"

His office looks similar to the way it was the first day of class. Except messier. There are pages strewn across the desk, the chairs, books stacked lying spine open to save the place.

"That will hurt the spines," I say, which is an inane comment.

He looks at the stack as if noticing it for the

first time. "Who hurt you, Anne?"

"Isn't it kind of late to be grading papers?"

"Answer the question."

Tears threaten, but I refuse to let them fall. I didn't lie to him at the hotel. I haven't cried in years, no matter how hard my father hit me. And I'm not about to start now that I found out my mother lied to me. "Can we not talk about it?"

"Was it Brandon?"

"What? No." Brandon might be a cheating ass, but he's not abusive. "It wasn't anyone on campus, okay? Forget about it. Are you working on another book?"

He runs a hand through his hair and sighs. "God, Anne."

"I've never flown a kite."

Dark eyebrows rise. "You looked me up."

"The library had *Behind the Bard.*"

He looks like he's fighting himself. I'm not going to talk about the bruise. In fact, I can't. Maybe he senses that, because he relents. "A kite's easy enough if you have good wind."

"I'm not even sure I know what good wind would be."

"That's because we're in the city."

I prop myself on his desk, nudging the papers gently aside so I don't mess up their position. It looks like chaos, but I have this feeling he knows where everything is. There's a method to his madness. And I should not find that so erotic.

"So," I say, dropping my messenger bag at my feet. "Are you finally going to tell me why you hate Tanglewood so much?"

His lips quirk, emphasizing his darkened jaw. It makes him look dangerous. And sensual. "I only meant because the buildings change the wind. They either block it altogether or create a wind tunnel. Neither is good for kite flying."

"Hmm," I say, letting my question stand.

"An answer for an answer."

He wants to trade? I don't know what he'd want to know about me. Then again, do I really care? My life has been pretty uninteresting. "Deal."

He moves to look out the window, which has reverse blinds, the kind that go up instead of down. That way people in offices can have relative privacy while still glimpsing the sun. Or in this case, the sunset. It's not summer, but the color gradients remind me of the cocktail I drank.

Purples, reds, yellows.

They paint his face with emotion.

"I can't tell you everything," he says. "Because it's not my story to tell. But I grew up in

Tanglewood. My father loved Shakespeare. He would have been a professor, a world-renowned professor, but...he wasn't well. He had these episodes. He'd disappear for months and come back with no shoes and no money. The city wasn't kind to people like him."

Sadness weighs on me. "I'm sorry."

"My brothers and I grew up wild. Our version of wild, anyway. We had his library. His texts and treatises. We also had drugs and sex and whatever other coping mechanisms we could find with no one to stop us."

"What about your mother?"

"She still teaches at Cambridge, actually. Hasn't retired."

"She *left* you here?"

"The irony is that her specialty is neurogenetics. Sometimes I think my father was like a pet project for her. That my brothers and I were like her own personal petri dish."

"Oh God."

He looks over, his eyes opaque. "I think you know something about shitty parents."

I raise my chin. "It's still your turn."

"Right," he says with a soundless laugh. "I got a scholarship to Tanglewood University, got my undergrad degree here. Left as soon as I got accepted to Yale for my PhD."

"What about Brandon?"

There's a flicker in his expression. "He wasn't...planned. Arabella got pregnant in her freshman year. We weren't even dating, but her family was very traditional. And powerful. They wanted her to get married."

I know times have changed, but... "And you agreed?"

His eyes are remote. "I was young and...selfish. I didn't want a baby. They wanted to control his upbringing, and I thought, why not? Everyone wins that way. It's not like I knew a damn thing about parenting. He'd grow up better without me."

My chest tightens. "Will."

"As I grew older, I realized my mistake. I tried to be there for him, but even then it was from another city. I swore I'd never come back to Tanglewood. It's always felt like a cursed place." A rough laugh. "Yet here I am. Life has a way of proving us wrong."

"Why did you come back?"

"I came to fulfill a debt. As quickly as possible so I could leave again. I wasn't supposed to get attached, not to anyone. Especially not to a student."

I suck in a breath. It's a declaration, isn't it? "What kind of debt?"

"The kind that can never really be repaid. Now it's my turn."

"For what?"

"For a question."

"Oh. That."

"Yes," he says, faintly mocking. "That. You hoped I would forget."

"It was my dad, okay? Big surprise. I'm a cliché of a scholarship student."

"You're not a cliché, dear heart. You're intelligent and curious and so damned special you can't even see it." He pauses. "But that isn't the question I was going to ask."

"What? No fair."

"It's perfectly fair. Here's my actual question: what is your favorite food?"

A simple question. At least it would be coming from anyone else. But now that I've read the opening of his book, now that he knows I have, it means something more. More than liking a particular spice or flavor. It's a way of sharing something deeper.

"Pancakes," I admit, mouth watering as I can almost taste the salt and butter melting over the top. "I don't even like the syrup. Just the pancakes, made a certain way."

"Hmm," he says, letting his question stand.

Shit. The memories come back to me, of scratched wooden furniture and pilling throw blankets. Of comfort. Of cleanliness. "My best friend in elementary school was named Tiffany. I used to walk to her house before school." I make a face. "I'd watch cartoons on their TV and eat the breakfast her mom made like a freeloader, but her mom never complained."

He watches me in that steady way, seeing too much.

"She would make it a certain way, sort of tan in the middle, then yellow with butter around the edges. Then tipped into a crispy brown edge that was my favorite part. I wouldn't even add syrup to mine. I loved the salt of it, the way it would fill my stomach for hours."

"Anne."

"It made me feel like I had a home."

Sorrow darkens his expression. "*Anne.*"

"Like I said." My voice comes out thicker. "I'm a cliché."

"Let me hold you."

"No." Holding me would mean showing weakness. It would mean falling deeper into the forbidden emotional abyss. I don't want that from

Professor Stratford. Couldn't survive it. But I can take something else from him, another form of solace. "Sit down."

A vintage brass lamp, its shade adorned with intricate patterns, provides illumination, casting intriguing shadows across the room. A worn Persian rug covers the floor, its intricate patterns softened by age and wear. Behind the desk, an imposing high-backed leather chair stands sentinel, its cracked surface bearing the marks of countless years of use.

He glances at the leather chair. "Sit down," he repeats.

I can't take sympathy. Can't he see that? "I want you to…make me forget."

For a moment it seems as if he might argue.

Then his lids lower, and I know I've won.

Or maybe I'm lost.

I'm not sure how to tell the difference any-more.

"You want to suck my cock?" he asks, his voice low.

I shiver. "I…yes. I do."

"Do you need another lesson?" It's a gentle taunt. "Have you had a hard cock in your mouth? Have you drunk a man down, made him lose control?"

A hard swallow. "Ye-es."

He sits down, leaning back in the high leather chair, making it creak. "Tell me about it."

Shame is a burning flame inside me. It stokes the arousal higher. "With Brandon."

He freezes, and for a moment I think it might be over. That the impasse of our connection to his son will break us apart. Then he cocks his head. "Did you like it?"

My cheeks burn. "Not really."

His voice is impossibly soft. "No?"

"He…he asked me to do it. I didn't really want to." Didn't really feel turned on, though I didn't know that at the time. We'd just made out, but I hadn't felt the heat between my legs. Hadn't even known I could feel like that until the night of the hotel room. "But I didn't want to have sex with him, either. And it seemed like a good compromise."

His eyes narrow. "My son acts like a boy. Not a man."

I shiver. "I'm not sure I did it right. I didn't know—"

"I'll teach you, dear heart," he murmurs. "Get down on your hands and knees."

I hesitate a moment. A globe, its colors faded with time, sits atop a wooden pedestal in one corner, while a framed portrait of a stern-looking academic hangs on the wall nearby. The office is steeped in intellectual tradition and honor.

I'm defiling it.

That fact shouldn't make me wetter.

I sink onto the plush old rug, still fully clothed.

He pats his thigh, similar to the way you'd call a dog. "Come."

My breath catches, and I crawl over to him, feeling both debased and revered.

"Good girl," he says when I reach him. He runs a hand over my hair and down my cheek. Then he leans back, putting his hands behind his head, making it clear who will be doing the work. "Now open my pants. Take me out. Find out how hard you've made me."

Brandon had undone his jeans in the dark back seat of the car. It's nothing like trying to undo the buckle of a leather belt and tug a zipper that's taut over an imposing erection. When I finally get him out, his cock springs up, ruddy and proud and damp at the tip. It's startling enough that I jump back. I've seen him before, haven't I? Though I'm not sure that I have, now that I think about it. Maybe only in shadow and feeling. I've certainly never been a handful of inches away, never realized how *large* it is. How intimidating.

How did this fit inside me?

How am I going to put it in my mouth?

"Hold it in your fist," he says, using that dark professor tone, both commanding and instructive. "Wrap your little fingers around it and pull."

He throbs in my hand, and I gasp.

A drop of liquid pearls at the top. "Lick me."

I do, tasting salt and man. Forbidden desire. He tastes different from Brandon. More spiced. More nuanced. More mature, though that might be lust-colored glasses.

"Good girl," he mutters. "Open wide. Suck on the head. Make me nice and wet. I want it dripping down the sides, making your fingers slick."

A moan escapes me as I obey, sucking on the large head like it's a savory lollipop. He bares his teeth, a feral expression that makes me suction him harder.

"Fuck," he groans. "You look so pretty like that, your lips wrapped around my cock. You were made for this, weren't you? Not for some punk-ass college kid. Not for a compromise. You were made to kneel and take a man down your throat. Weren't you?"

Desire veils my vision, making everything hazy. I moan in agreement around his cock, and he flexes in my mouth as if he could feel the vibration. I hum again, just to be sure.

His breath catches. "Always a gifted student. Now slide your fist down and then up. Down and then up. Again. Do it while you suck me. Yes, that's it. That's the way. What a good girl. What a good fucking girl on your knees, your ass in the air, your lips wide."

How must I look, behind and almost under his desk? Filthy.

"Use your tongue now, right there—ahh, God. Right there. Yes."

I'm lost in the rhythm, lost in the groans and grunts he makes, the unlikely power of this situation. I might be on my knees, but he's completely enraptured by my tongue, held captive by my mouth, enthralled by my fist.

He puts a hand on my head, clenching in my hair. "I'm coming. God. Swallow me down. Understand? Don't lose a drop."

My fist speeds up of its own accord, and he comes with a hard, quick shout, spilling his cum into my mouth, a burst of salt and bitterness on my tongue. I swallow with eager obedience, wanting to please him—as both my professor and my lover.

His fist in my hair holds me there, rocks me through the final spurts, keeps me there to catch every single drop until he finally slips from my lips.

I'm still catching my breath when he drags me onto his lap. My legs are spread wide. Any shame or uncertainty I felt has long fled. I only want relief now, relief from the raging arousal, from the heavy heartbeat I feel in my clit.

He picks up a thick black pen with a silver clip. "Do you know who gave me this?" he asks, and I can only moan uselessly in response. "The dean. It was a gift when I agreed to come work here at Tanglewood, when I agreed to help. An expensive gift, really. It costs as much as an entire semester course at the university."

Despite my need, my eyes widen. That's a lot for a *pen*. "Please."

He smiles, but it's not a kind smile. No, it's savage. It's rude and cruel, like Shakespeare wrote. He puts the cool, smooth barrel of the pen against my clit, and I jerk my hips, desperate for friction. It's hard, though, on such a small surface. Thick for a pen, but small compared to the pressure of him, of his cock, of what I really need.

He knows that. God, he knows. That's why

he looks satisfied.

"Fuck it," he murmurs.

And I have no choice. My hips thrust, seeking, searching, finding only the barest pressure. My breasts feel swollen, pushing against my top, and he watches them bounce through the clothes. "It's not enough," I whimper.

"No?" he asks, his confusion not quite genuine. "Then perhaps this."

He inserts the pen, bottom side up inside me, sliding it into my clenching channel. The side covered by the cap is in his hand as he thrusts it gently inside me. The feel of the pen, so much cooler than his fingers or his cock, makes me shiver. Then his thumb fingers my clit, and I sob out my relief. "Yes, yes, yes."

"That's it," he murmurs. "Come for me, dear heart."

I can do nothing but obey. Stars burst behind my eyes as my hips move mindlessly, pleasure a shock to my system, a hard reboot, a clench strong enough to leave me gasping at the end, my mouth open against the warm linen of his white button-down.

In the aftermath he produces a handkerchief, which he uses to wipe clean first the pen and then the opening of my body. I'm pliant, still tender from the aftershocks of orgasm as he straightens my clothes and then his. The pen returns to his desk, its black shining surface innocuous after what happened, after I climaxed around it.

He studies me, his expression enigmatic. "You shouldn't have come here, Ms. Hill."

A shiver runs through me at the sudden, uncrossable distance between us.

Make me forget. That's what I requested, and it worked, it worked. It worked for the eternity that I had him in my mouth, an endless expanse of arousal. But now that I'm on the other side of the desk, it comes rushing back, unwelcome and cold.

Hurt swirls inside me, along with the latent suspicion I've had of him.

It turns into a fire inside me.

One that makes me bold enough to ask, "Are you in the Shakespeare Society?"

He stiffens. "Why would you think that?"

"I don't know. Because you were at the masquerade ball. And because someone invited me to join the society as a member, so I thought maybe it was you."

"Someone invited you?"

I pull the black cardstock from my messenger bag. "Someone left this for me at my dorm. At least I think it was meant for me. It's not addressed to anyone."

He reads it, his expression darkening. "There's no date or time."

"Or location. But I was reading up on secret societies and one of them had a puzzle you had to solve before you could join. I wonder if..." I shrug. "I don't know. It sounds silly when I say it out loud, but there might be invisible ink. Or some kind of QR code embedded. Or who knows? I'll work on it more tonight."

"No."

"What do you mean, no?"

He rips the invitation in two. And then four.

My mouth drops open. "What the *hell*? That was mine."

"That was dangerous. You aren't to go anywhere near the Shakespeare Society. Forget you ever heard about them. And do *not* go looking for them."

"You had no right to do that. It was my invitation. And who are you to talk about danger when you were at the masquerade?"

"I was there to make sure the students were safe."

"Is that what you call it?" The memory of that empty classroom fills the air between us, the slap of his hand on my ass, the slide of his tongue on my clit.

He tries to modulate his voice. "I'm serious, Anne. The Shakespeare Society is bad news. Stay away from them." His expression darkens. "And stay away from my office."

My eyes narrow. "You can call me Ms. Hill. Let's get one thing straight, Professor Stratford. You can give me assignments in class, but you don't control me outside that room."

I turn and leave, rushing headlong into a burgeoning drizzle.

CHAPTER TWENTY-THREE

Scavenger Hunt

I EMAIL THE dean, telling him about the invitation and all the marks I can remember about it. He replies with a short thank-you note, asking me to keep him apprised. Thankfully he doesn't ask to see it, since the pieces are in Professor Stratford's office.

My bruise fades. The weeks pass in a blur of studying and exams. I'm still pissed at Will, but he doesn't seem particularly apologetic, acting stern and remote during class.

Schoolwork marches on, unconcerned with my personal angst.

That's how I end up asleep with my face pressed into a book, the page bent, creating a crease in my cheek. My hands rub the ridge gently as I try to remember how I got here.

I was working on my literature essay.

A knock on the door makes me jump. It sounds urgent, like maybe they already knocked. That's probably what woke me up.

I rub my eyes and open the door, expecting that Daisy forgot her key card.

Instead it's Lorelei.

"Where's Bradshaw? It's an hour past curfew."

Oh shit. "She went…"

There's nothing good to say here.

Even if she were at the one library on campus that stays open until midnight studying, it would violate the rules. It's a Wednesday night. No reason that she should be off campus. No reason not to make it back for curfew.

"I'm going to write her up."

"Wait. I'll find her. I'll bring her back."

"Then there will be *two* students missing."

"Please. I'm sure she's in one of the libraries that stay open late studying. Or maybe in those computer labs. You know engineering students and their obsession with green text on black screens."

"No," she says, her tone frigid. "I don't."

"Well, they love it." And I've got to find a way to fix this for my friend. "Or maybe she got caught in all this rain. A campus bus might have broken down. Anything."

"How is that my problem?" Lorelei asks, her tone icy.

"It's not, but…please. Give me time to find her."

A pause while she studies me from behind her winged liner. "Fine. You have one hour."

"Thank you, thank you, thank you."

The first thing I do is call Daisy's phone. It's too much to hope that she answers. *I'm right outside the door.* I can imagine her saying that with a smile on her face and then breezing inside. She might have even convinced Lorelei to come scare the shit out of me. That's the kind of prank she'd pull. Then we'd laugh.

I wish that were happening.

"Daisy, it's me," I tell her voicemail. "Lorelei is pissed. Where are you?"

After hanging up, I send a text asking the same question.

No answer.

The little checkmark next to the message stays hollow, meaning she hasn't read it.

I open the application that shows me her location. She's on campus, it says. That's a relief. I zoom in with my fingers so I can figure out where. The buildings are marked by solid colors while the walkways are outlined. My head cocks to the side. Based on the landmarks, this is the building where my class with Professor Stratford is. This is the place where I sucked his cock. Where he held my head, groaning his pleasure, shouting my name.

The little blue dot shows her outside the building.

Where it's definitely raining.

What could she be doing there? That's a humanities building. She doesn't have classes there. And even if she did, there's no reason to be there late on a Wednesday night.

Or standing outside in the rain.

I throw on some sandals, because my canvas slippers will get drenched in a second. I pull a Tanglewood University hoodie over my head, shove my key card and phone into my pocket. Then I'm speed-walking through the rain. Part of me wants to run, because why the hell hasn't she texted me back already? The slick rain makes it hard to move quickly. The last thing I need to do is slip and land face-first in a puddle.

I've been to this building a bunch of times, but it looks different in the dark. Rain forms a curtain around me, blocking anything farther than five feet away. Rain slides down my phone's screen as I get closer and closer to the blue dot.

Then I'm standing there, basically in the same place. Except, of course, there's no one here. No Daisy. No anyone.

Only a closed-up coffee cart.

I find myself looking in the bushes like an absolute idiot. Did Daisy drop her phone somewhere? She could at this very moment be back at the dorm. Or maybe it's some kind of tech glitch, throwing her signal fifty yards from her actual location.

Then I spot it—underneath the cart.

I reach under and pull out her phone, complete with its case covered in daisies.

There's also a white card that says: 52nd and Trinity St.

Those are two streets on campus. I recognize the names, if not the specific corner.

Is this a scavenger hunt?

I flip the card over, revealing a faint imprint of a hand holding a skull. Shit. It *is* a scavenger hunt, one being put on by the Shakespeare Society. I want to believe that Daisy is in on the prank, but it's hard to imagine her risking getting written up and her entire scholarship just to be part of some secret society. Also hard to imagine her giving up her phone for even an hour.

What's the alternative? That they're holding

her against her will?

I shiver.

The address is on the other side of campus. I head in the opposite direction, because it takes me to a bus stop. There are free campus shuttles that drive in circles. They run a little slower at night, but I still get there faster than walking in the slippery dark.

The bus driver doesn't look up as I get on, dripping wet on the metal floor. There's no one else on the bus. He still stops at every single bench, picking up no one. My teeth are chattering beneath the blast of AC. I'm drenched.

When we're close, I hop off and rush to the corner.

Where there's...nothing.

More looking under bushes. I find the piece of paper at the top of the stone steps of a darkened building. There are no words on this one. Only an arrow pointing up. I look up, where a sign reads *The Baldwin Building*. The one named after Brandon's grandmother.

What does it mean?

I sure as hell hope they don't expect me to climb the building in the rain, because that is definitely not happening. I'm about one second from giving up and going back to the dorm room.

I'm going to curse Daisy out once I find her.

Unless she's in trouble.

No, I have to see this through.

Think.

The building is owned by the business department, I think. I've never even been inside. Funny, because my best friend and the coffee cart *did* have a connection to me. This building doesn't. Unless the only connection is the name itself.

What if I need to find Brandon?

I mutter a curse under my breath.

At this time of night he's probably at his frat house.

My jeans are fully waterlogged and dragging down my hips, my eyes stinging from what is probably acid rain by the time I use the knocker on the heavy door. It's opened by some guy I don't recognize, presumably one of the new recruits from this year.

He stares at me blankly. "You selling something?"

"Brandon," I gasp out.

The door shuts in my face. I'm on the verge of knocking again when the door opens. Brandon is there. Shock crosses his face at my appearance. He grabs my wrist and pulls me inside. "Why are you so wet?"

"It's raining," I say, stating the obvious. "Where's Daisy?"

He looks at me like I grew horns. "In your dorm room, probably?"

My teeth chatter in the cool foyer. From far away I can hear the sounds of male laughter and explosions that are hopefully coming from a TV. "No. She's not there. I got this note. This welcome card. And then they had her phone. And then your grandmother."

I'm not making any sense, too cold to speak clearly, but he gets it anyway. He grins. "The Shakespeare Society. I told them you were cool. I got you in."

"Okay. Great. Can you get me *out*?"

"What are you talking about? They have parties and shit."

"They kidnapped Daisy."

His face goes blank. It makes him look even younger. "What?"

"Listen, I don't know for sure. Maybe she's in on this whole thing. But I don't think so. She wouldn't have left her phone outside. She wouldn't have missed curfew. And she wouldn't have made me run around in the freaking rain, terrified for her."

His eyebrows draw together. "It's a test, right?"

"A dangerous one."

Unease moves through him. "No, I mean. They like to have a good time. Maybe sometimes they go a little far, but they wouldn't hurt Daisy."

"Then help me find her."

He spreads his hands. "I don't know where she is."

"You said you know them."

"I've met them. I'm not part of their inner circle."

I push past him. People stop playing pool to stare at the drenched crazy lady, but I ignore them and pound the stairs to what I remember as Brandon's room. Sure enough there's a white card on his windowsill. He followed me up. I shove it in his face. "What's this?"

"I don't know." He looks a little panicked now. "I swear I don't."

The only thing written on it is a square with a much smaller circle inside it. "What does this mean? Some kind of geometry thing? Maybe engineering?"

He bites his lip, thinking.

My brain flips through every symbol I've ever seen. This is one of those times when a not-quite photographic memory would come in handy. Except I can't find anything. "We learned about the symbol for alchemy in Professor Miller's class. It's a square inside of a circle. Maybe it's that but inverted somehow."

"You're too smart."

"Oh my God." We had this argument way too many times when we were dating. He hated that I was so focused on school, even though he knew my scholarship depended on it.

"No," he says, shaking his head. "I mean you're thinking too deep. Look at it. They're sending you around campus, right? What's the biggest square?"

"The quad," I say, meeting his eyes. "With the big circular fountain."

We take off. I've lost any sense of decorum, any sense of self-preservation. I'm sliding on the pebbled walkways, but I won't be able to relax until I find her.

I'm panting by the time we reach the quad. It's also empty. At least it seems that way. The heavy sheets of rain make it hard to see. It feels bigger like this. As if it takes two years to traverse. Then we're at the fountain.

"Oh fuck," he says.

The spray of water blocks my view. I circle it and then I see her. Daisy lies half in the water, her head resting on concrete, her eyes closed. A thin white dress clings to her pale skin, making her look...dead. I rush to her and pull her out of the fountain. "Help me," I snap to Brandon, and he pulls himself from his shock to help me set her on the ground.

Rain falls in her open mouth.

I press my fingers to her pulse. It's there. Thready and soft, but there.

"Daisy," I shout, but she doesn't move. What have they done to her? No way in hell did she choose this. She could have drowned in that fountain.

One slip on the rain-slicked stone ledge, and she would have been underwater.

I shake her, panicked. "Daisy!"

Her eyes flutter. "Who? Annie?"

"Yes. It's me. I'm here. You're going to be okay."

She gives me a faint smile, which would be more reassuring if her lips didn't look tinted blue. "I knew you'd find me." Then her eyes close.

"Call for help," I tell Brandon, but when I turn to him, he already has his phone pressed to his ear. "Campus security. Or 9-1-1. I don't know, just someone."

His expression is grim as whoever's on the other end answers. "Hi, Dad."

CHAPTER TWENTY-FOUR

Provost's House

THERE ARE A few places where faculty can live on campus. There's a particularly grim set of one-bedroom apartments, usually used by first-year adjunct professors moving from out of state. Provosts are given nicer homes, old-fashioned Georgian structures. Part of the reason they're given that space is so that they can host events. I've been to such things. One for my scholarship ceremony. Another when I attended a violinist's small salon. There were canapes and flutes of champagne and an abundance of blazers on both men and women.

It's in one of these homes where Professor Stratford lives, apparently.

He carries Daisy there, his expression severe.

"Shouldn't we bring her to a hospital?"

That earns me a dark look. "They'll call her

family."

I press my lips together. Shit shit shit.

Even if they weren't already pressuring her to stay home and make babies, this would push them over the edge. How could she advocate for herself in this state? We are over eighteen years old, but I've already seen that the world still treats us like children. They expect our parents to help pay for college and to support us...and if they don't? Too bad.

He passes the living room and moves into the hallway. A small bedroom contains a small bed with white sheets and bare walls. He sets her down, and I fuss with the blankets, pulling them up, trying to warm her cold skin.

The front of his white button-down has become damp where he carried Daisy's body, the fabric almost translucent, revealing dark ink. I remember noticing the beautifully scripted words at the hotel, but I couldn't read them then. With the shirt covering him, I still can't.

It's a reminder that I don't really know him, this man. My lover. My secret.

My professor.

"Try to make her comfortable until the doctor comes," he says.

"What doctor?"

"Someone I trust."

Okay. I guess that's enough for me. Except. "Who did this?"

His expression is dark and severe. "Don't you know?"

"I mean, the Shakespeare Society. But *why* would they do this?"

He sighs. "It's a form of initiation. A test that you have to pass to get in. That's what they usually are. Dangerous or degrading activities."

"So they kidnapped her, risked her life for a freaking scavenger hunt?"

He doesn't blink. "Yes."

"That's the most fucked-up thing I've ever heard."

"I warned you, Anne. I told you to stay away from them."

"I did," I say, but abruptly remember that I talked to Dean Morris after that.

Not that it did any good. Is that why they punished me? Then again, an initiation isn't precisely a punishment. It's a twisted form of welcome.

My voice is bitter as I ask the final question. "Does that mean I'm *in* the society now?"

He doesn't answer, because he's already gone down the hallway, presumably to find the doctor.

I make myself useful, removing the thin wet shift from her body and tucking her under the blankets. She wakes up during this process, her blue eyes bleary. "Did you find me?"

That makes me sob a laugh. "Yes, sweetheart. I found you."

"Oh good."

Then she's asleep again.

This is the flaw in Alyssa's logic, I realize now. Because the university may not be responsible for every person on its campus. But it didn't require us to run a gauntlet to attend. No one was tossed into a fountain and left to drown. That's not to say they only have our best interests at heart. They're a business intent on making money.

At worst, the university is indifferent.

The Shakespeare Society is actively cruel.

Savage, extreme, rude, cruel. The words flit through my mind.

They apply to desire. And to the society.

Someone arrives, though he doesn't look like any doctor I've ever seen. His blond hair looks almost white with the rain, but his unlined face tells me he isn't very old. Especially for a doctor. I want someone with gray hair and a hundred wrinkles.

I block the doorway. "How do I know you're

not some quack?"

"Anders Sorenson, M.D. I have hospital privileges at Tanglewood General as well as North Shore. I've won awards and done two tours with Doctors without Borders, but I think the most useful credential is my ability to keep my mouth shut."

After a long moment, I move aside.

He seems professional enough as he examines her, using a stethoscope and other tools from his black bag.

Oh God. I won't be back within that hour Lorelei gave me.

Then again, missing curfew could be the least of our problems.

Another thought occurs to me. I turn to Professor Stratford, who looks grim. "She won't get in trouble for this, will she? They won't blame her for playing a prank or something?"

His ebony eyes are luminous in the darkened room. "I don't know."

Professors are supposed to know everything. Every nuance. Every academic paper. They're supposed to have all the answers. If he doesn't know, we're screwed.

Anders gestures us into the hallway. "Her vitals are strong. That's the most important thing.

If I had to guess, she was drugged. Rohypnol, something like that."

Horror closes my throat. "The date rape drug?"

Anders looks solemn, his pale blue eyes both eerie and calming. He exudes confidence. And experience. I wonder how many late-night calls he's received connected to illicit activities. "I did a cursory exam and don't see any signs of assault, sexual or otherwise. Though that doesn't mean it didn't happen."

"Oh God."

"If she were in a hospital, they'd give her saline solution in an IV and watch her overnight. If you're going to keep her here, try to make her take sips of water. Not gulps. Not entire cups. Just sips every few hours. Keep her in bed. I suspect she'll wake up with a killer headache in the morning, and maybe some memory loss. If it's worse than that, call me again."

Then he's gone, and I stare into the darkened bedroom while Will shows the doctor out. And presumably pays him something. How do secret doctor house calls even work?

Something compels me to follow him out. I kneel on the balcony like a spy, watching Professor Stratford. He's removed his wet shirt and is now wearing a black T-shirt with jeans.

He's talking with two people.

One I recognize as Professor Cormac Stratford, Will's brother.

The other is an elegant blonde woman from my Cultural and Social Anthropology class, the one I wrote the essay on omens and prophecies for. Professor Avery Miller is a renowned scholar on Greek mythology and something of a personal hero of mine. She wrote a book on Helen of Troy that changed the narrative on beauty and feminine agency. Her own beauty and natural elegance would make her unapproachable, but she's also surprisingly kind.

"They have to be stopped," she's saying.

She must be talking about the Shakespeare Society. Cormac mutters something about Dean Morris. He makes a slashing motion with his hand.

Will curses. "No one knows a damn thing."

I creep back into the spare bedroom where Daisy still sleeps. We've slept in the same room for a long time. She looks almost peaceful, if I didn't know what happened to her.

It should make me feel better that the professors are working on bringing the society down, but it doesn't. It's too late for her. Too late to help. And it's all my fault. I may not have asked to be part of the society, but I wanted it. I wanted to belong so damn bad that I caused this.

I stay by her side all night, my guilt a third person in the room.

It's pale dawn when I open my eyes. She's already sitting up in bed.

"Daisy," I say, moving slowly, sleep still weighing me down. "What happened? Are you okay? We can take you to the hospital, but I wasn't sure…"

"God, no," she says, sounding almost normal. "You did the right thing."

"We're at the provost's house. Will lives here."

One eyebrow rises. "Will?"

I blush. "Professor Stratford. What do you remember from last night?"

"They grabbed me when I was leaving my last class. A white van. A black hood over my head." She rolls her eyes, but even I can see she's shaken. "So stereotypical. I mean, where's the creativity? If you're going to do Shakespeare, I expect a cape and dagger or something."

"There was a doctor. He said he thought you might have been drugged." I swallow hard. "Did they hurt you? We can take you to a hospital, get you tested. Especially now that you're awake, you can tell them not to call your family."

She cringes. "Unnecessary."

"But—"

"No, seriously. I've woken up from keg parties feeling worse than this. I just want to go back to our room. Forget that this ever happened."

"We can't just go to class like everything is normal."

"What should we do instead?"

"I don't know! Figure out who took you. Call the cops. Make them pay."

"Mmm, as much as I love the idea of being a lady vigilante, I feel like that would interfere with my sleep routine. I need a solid eight hours a night to maintain all of this." She draws her hand under her face in a model pose.

Even pale and exhausted, she looks lovely.

And vulnerable. So freaking vulnerable.

They could have done anything to her in that van. She could have died in the fountain.

My voice shakes. "Don't you want to know why this happened?"

"I already know why," she murmurs.

I can barely meet her blue-sky eyes. "It's because of me."

"Anne—"

"It was some kind of insane initiation." My

throat feels tight, but I can't stop the confession. "Like a puzzle for me to solve to get inducted into the Shakespeare Society."

Her voice is gentle. So is her hand when it takes mine. "I know."

"So it's my fault. You see? My fault this happened to you."

"Were you in the van? Did you drug me?"

"Of course not but—"

"Then it's not your fault."

I press my eyes together, hating the sting. *Don't cry.* "Why don't you hate me?"

"What a bunch of egomaniacs do doesn't reflect on you. I knew you'd look for me. I knew you'd find me. You're my bestie."

My chest tightens. "You're my bestie, too."

"So, let's forget about this."

Despite what she says, I don't think either of us is going to forget this anytime soon. But I want to let her recover in peace. "You know what I was thinking about? When the dorms close for winter, what if instead of us going back to our houses, we sublet an apartment? It'll be tough money-wise, but we can get a studio, just one room. We're already used to sharing the space."

She manages a wan smile. "I have a lead on jobs as elves at the winter market."

"I was going to suggest we go back to Cressida City, but that's even better."

"I thought you were never going to do that again."

It feels like a hundred years ago since I made that declaration, fresh from my night with a handsome stranger, my pockets flush with cash. I wasn't ashamed of what I'd done, but I didn't want to do it again. Since then I've seen how much farther we can fall.

"I'm not letting you marry your freaking uncle."

"And I don't want you to have to go back to your lying bastard parents."

"So it's settled. You and me. This winter."

"I'd make a great elf," she says with a long, tensile yawn. "Very hot."

CHAPTER TWENTY-FIVE
Manifest Destiny

I KNOW WHAT my essay will be about now.

It takes me long hours to write it, which I spend in the library. Partly that's because I need more room to spread out than the tiny desk in the dorm room.

Mostly it's because it depresses Daisy to see me doing schoolwork. The school counselor offered to help her have the semester dropped from her transcript. That way she doesn't have to cram for finals while she's recovering.

In a way I understand it. And I'm grateful that the university cares enough to let her do that. But I can't help but feel like she's giving up, like this is going to change her life.

Someone slides into the seat across the study table.

I look up from my laptop to see Tyler wearing

a Tanglewood University jersey. "Hey. You working on the comparative analysis essay?"

"Almost done."

"What did you decide on?"

I hesitate, wondering if he might mock me, but I'm not ashamed of my topic. "A certain pop star who was placed in a conservatorship and her boyfriend."

His eyebrows rise. "I figured you'd go for something more...you know?"

More what? "Not really."

"Like someone is doing Pocahontas and John. Someone else is doing this couple from one of those science fiction shows. Star Tunes or Star Truck or something."

"Do you actually not know *Star Trek* or are you just messing with me?"

"Star Trout? Are there fish in space?"

I have to laugh at his confused expression. "Asshole."

"Nerd," he says with some affection. "So these pop stars. They didn't actually die or anything. They just broke up. Does that really count as a tragedy?"

"Well, I hope Professor Stratford thinks so, otherwise I'm toast."

"If you're writing it, I'm sure he's going to say

it's the most insightful idea ever."

I freeze, wondering if we gave ourselves away somehow. Could he tell from how Professor Stratford talks to me? Or the way I looked at him? "Why?"

"Because you're a genius," he says, as if I'm dumb.

"Oh, that."

"Oh, that," he says, teasing. "Can I read it?"

I blink down at the pile of books spread out on the table. Some are about Shakespeare and literary analysis. Others about the history of musicians. There are too many to move, so I hand over my laptop so that he can read my essay.

The pop star's fight for agency and subsequent decades spent buried beneath the thumb of her family makes a clear enough line to Juliet.

Romeo was the trickier one. He'd originally gotten fame and glory after their breakup, particularly while claiming the victim. He went on to cheat on multiple subsequent girlfriends while attempting to elevate himself with damning songs about them. It seemed to be a pattern, one that worked for a while. Until it didn't.

It's a career that many men would envy, but one that has never seemed to satisfy a man intent on stepping on anyone and everyone. And that is a form of suicide.

He destroyed his own dreams.

Tyler looks up, eyebrows raised. "Impressive."

"Thanks. What's yours about?"

"Tom and Jerry. You know, the cartoon."

I can't help my lips twitching. "That's pretty good."

"Yeah, I thought about the Road Runner and Wile E. Coyote, but there's something more fatalistic about a cat and mouse being enemies in the natural order."

"I can't actually remember. Did they…love each other?"

"A great question," he says in a grave voice, his eyes twinkling. "I cited multiple instances of one of them expressing genuine concern over the other when they'd get hurt. It was only society that placed them in their roles—Tom, whose job as a house cat was literally to catch mice. And Jerry who was only trying to survive in his little mouse hole."

"It's not like he could live somewhere else. We build houses on the habitats where mice and other animals lived and then get mad at them for being there."

"Ooh, that's a good point. Manifest destiny as applied to mice. I'm adding that in."

I grin. "You know, I'm glad we sat next to each other the first day."

"Me too. Even though you dismissed me as a dumb jock."

Guilt makes me cringe. "You noticed that?"

"It's this handsome face. What else are you going to think?"

"Such humility."

"That's okay. I thought I hit it off with Daisy, but then she never called me back."

"She's had a lot going on."

"I heard…rumors. Not that I always believe them or anything."

I look down, then back at him. "You were at the masquerade ball."

"Now that was a fucking party."

"Are you…part of the Shakespeare Society?"

A snort. "Not likely. You aren't the only one who assumes I'm a dumb jock."

"Good," I say, a little too sharply. "They're dangerous."

His brows draw together. "Did they hurt her?"

Did they hurt her? I don't even know what they did to her.

She was only gone a few hours in total. There were no bruises on her body. No breaks or fractures. Those would be easier to fix, I think. The damage happened inside her mind.

She seems listless. Unmoored. "Yes."

He curses, looking away. "Sometimes I don't know about this place. This whole fucking school. The arrogance. As if they can get away with anything."

"Aren't you part of them?"

"Aren't you?" he counters.

"I'm just the scholarship kid."

His laugh is only a little bitter. "Is that what you tell yourself? I hate to be the one to break it to you, but you belong here more than anyone. Which sometimes is a good thing. And other times, not so much."

He leaves me frowning over that pronouncement.

Have I been using my financial status as a way to maintain distance from the condescension here? Pretension is inherent to being a high-brow college. After all, there's no way to be exclusive if you include everyone.

Which would mean the Shakespeare Society isn't really counterculture.

It's simply an extension of the inherent elitism.

I love reading, love learning, love thinking,

but I can't deny that it's gotten more complicated since I got to Tanglewood. In my desperate desire to belong, have I become part of a machine designed to keep people out?

The university has a website used for submitting work, one whose timestamps are considered God when it comes to determining lateness. The essay is due at midnight, but I want to submit it now. That way I can focus on Daisy when I get back to the dorm room.

I click on the heading *Advanced Comparative Analysis of Literature*.

There's a small circular photo next to Professor William Stratford's name. He looks serious, my sheep farmer. Not as classically handsome as Tyler or even Brandon. His features are rougher, more severe. This small, his dark eyes hold no hint of blue. I can imagine him standing on green hills with wind whipping around him, a man working with his hands. Perhaps writing poetry in Gaelic at the end of the day. It's a romantic notion. A silly one.

And I can no longer deny that I'm falling for him.

That I've already fallen.

I press the button to upload my essay, holding my breath until I see the little green checkmark.

Here's hoping he likes my essay. Then I stand up and stretch, hearing multiple joints crack. Most of the books end up back in their respective shelves.

Then my messenger bag and I are heading back to the dorm.

I stop by the coffee shop to grab a chocolate croissant, Daisy's favorite. And I'm holding the bag as I slide the key card and step inside the room. "I come bearing gifts! Don't tell me you're not hungry, because hunger is not required to enjoy pastries."

The room doesn't answer me. It's empty.

Daisy's bed is usually messy, but now it's been perfectly made. The edges look surprisingly straight, like crisp corners made of bent paper. I have the random thought that she must have learned that bed-making technique back at her fundamentalist home.

We share a desk between our beds, one with drawers on either side.

My desk usually contains stacks of books. Hers usually contains little wires and doodads that she uses to build circuits, her books on the floor. But her desk is clear in sharp contrast to the clutter of mine. Her books are gone. My heart pounds.

Lorelei appears at the door I didn't quite close. "She left."

I blink, uncomprehending. "To go to another dorm room?"

There's genuine sympathy beneath the heavy eyeliner. "To go home."

"No," I whisper.

"She left you this." A folded piece of notebook paper ends up in my hand. "I would give you shit about not being your secretary right now, but you look like someone kicked your puppy. Sit down before you fall down."

She waits until I land heavily on my bed before closing the door behind her.

I open the notebook paper.

Don't worry about me. Seriously. Don't. I know you're still doing it, but I can't stay just for you. I need to go home. It's where I belong. I'm sorry.

My hand is shaking when I'm done reading.

Home, where her father's going to make her marry her uncle?

Home, where she'll have to obey and subjugate herself to survive?

Heat burns my eyes, but even now, trembling with worry for my best friend, I can't let myself cry. I would lose control. I would lose control of myself and never, ever get it back.

CHAPTER TWENTY-SIX

Instruments of Darkness

I'M ABOUT TO knock on the provost's door when I hear male voices inside. I duck back into the shadows, half-hidden behind bushes when the door opens, spilling yellow light onto the walkway. From this angle I can't see who's there, which hopefully means they can't see me.

"Thank you for your service to the university." I recognize Dean Morris's voice. "Now that the Shakespeare Society is cleaned up, students will be safer."

"Of course." Professor Stratford. "It was my duty."

My eyes widen from my hidden perch. The Shakespeare Society is cleaned up? They only performed their twisted initiation ritual recently. I'm probably not the only new member, either. They aren't shut down. They're growing. So why would Professor Stratford say that? Why would he lie?

Their voices drop to murmurs. Then footsteps depart.

Every muscle in my body strains from holding myself still. I don't really want to talk to Professor Stratford now. Especially with this dawning suspicion. Why did I even come here?

"You can come out now," says a low voice.

Damn it. Caught.

I take a step into the light, blinking against the brightness. Professor Stratford's dark beauty appears haloed, handsome features pronounced, as if he's a fallen angel. "Um. Hi."

He pulls me inside, kisses me. "You shouldn't have come here."

"I'm sorry."

"Don't be." He presses me against the inside of the door. "I missed you."

My body melts, but my mind stays a degree removed. "Why did Dean Morris thank you for shutting down the society? It's not closed."

He pulls back, his expression veiled. "You heard that, hmm?"

"The debt had to do with the Shakespeare Society, didn't it? The reason why you came back?"

He pauses, runs a hand through his hair. "You're too damn smart," he says, his voice almost mild. "Yes. He called me to come back and help destroy it. Which we did."

"You did?"

"Yes, after Ms. Bradshaw's experience, I followed the clues until I found the students who were resurrecting the club. They're being expelled as we speak."

"Wow. So it's...over?" It doesn't feel over, but I suppose it could be. How would I know what he does when we're not together? How would I know who's being expelled?

"It's over." His gaze is tender, his touch gentle as he tucks a strand of hair behind my ear. "You were really afraid, weren't you?"

"For Daisy."

"Right. For Daisy."

My stomach turns over in grief and fear. "That's why... I guess that's why I came. To tell you that she dropped the semester. Went back home."

"She can come back in the spring."

Can she? Her father might not let her leave. She might be married and pregnant by the time next semester starts. Anxiety feels like a bird inside my rib cage. "Maybe."

"What about you?" he asks. "Are you going home when the semester ends?"

"I have to. The dorms close."

"And your father? The one who gave you that black eye?"

I shiver. "What should I do instead? Move into the provost's house?"

"Perhaps."

"Or maybe I can live in one of the underground bomb shelters."

"Is that what you'd like?"

"I'd like to be in your bed," I whisper. "I know I shouldn't have come, that I'm not supposed to be here, but I just want to forget for a little while."

He leads me down the hallway, past the empty guest room where Daisy had once been, into a larger bedroom drawn in leather and masculine colors. He tucks me into bed with undue care, as if I'm close to shattering. Maybe I am. His kiss on my forehead is warm and reassuring. He doesn't try to have sex with me, and despite the low hum of ever-present arousal when I'm around him, I almost like this better.

After all, his arms are the only place where I've ever really belonged.

He curls around me from behind, a profound

intimacy. It feels like the entire landscape of my life has crumbled under my feet, re-formed into something jagged and sharp. My mother doesn't have cancer. My best friend left school. The school itself is a dangerous place, instead of the haven I thought it would be.

Professor Stratford has been the only constant.

I fall into a heavy sleep, sinking, sinking, held only by his arms.

In my dreams I see a masculine hand holding a skull. I hear laughter. Dark eyes tinged with blue promise both retribution and reward. I wake up panting. Professor Stratford still sleeps beside me. Why would he be in my nightmare?

I should probably wake him up, let him distract me with pleasure.

Or maybe just sneak back to my dorm room.

The threat of being written up by Lorelei doesn't even scare me anymore. My scholarship felt like the fulcrum of all my hopes and dreams. Now it seems almost like an albatross.

The warm masculine scent of Will's body lulls me back to sleep.

My eyes are drifting shut as I notice the heavy ink. The black T-shirt he's wearing is thin and soft from washing. It's lifted in our sleep to reveal his muscled abs, along with his tattoo, the one I never got to read. I nudge the hem up another inch, revealing the beautiful calligraphy. *Infinite jest,* it says in an old-fashioned scroll, large loops beneath the *f* and the *j*.

My blood runs cold.

Infinite jest.

It means nothing. Probably. It's a famous phrase from Shakespeare. Professor Stratford studies and teaches Shakespeare. That's the only connection. It has nothing to do with the Shakespeare Society, which uses those words on their invitation.

Does it?

I gently move Will's heavy, lightly furred arm onto the cool sheets.

His white dress shirt drapes a nearby chair. I pull it around myself, closing one of the buttons. It hangs to the middle of my thighs. I have to roll the sleeves up.

It feels strange wandering the provost's house alone in the dark. I'm guessing the artwork belongs to the university. Most of them are paintings of the actual college or people who went here. Much like the office that came pre-filled with books, these spaces are meant for professors to use and then move on.

Only the office contains anything that might

belong to Will.

Half-opened cardboard boxes spill over with what looks like personal items.

I have no right to go through his things, of course. It's a violation of privacy. A crossing of boundaries. But something compels me to step deeper inside, to open a cardboard flap. Mystery has swirled around Professor Stratford from the beginning. Why did he return to the city? To destroy the Shakespeare Society, he said. And it's accomplished.

So why don't I completely believe him?

A thick leather-bound yearbook from decades ago lies on top. Flipping through the pages, I find a picture of a younger Will Stratford. He's just as handsome. Not smiling. There's something behind his eyes.

Something dark, angry, maybe even danger-ous.

I find a diploma, a class ring, and a faded program to a football game.

At the bottom is where I find the leather binder, black and thick, embossed with a hand holding a skull. Inside there's that familiar block lettering that I've seen at the front of the class-room. *Bend over the table.* It's Will's handwriting. There are listed positions, like in a club. Treasurer, Secretary, VP of Membership. There are names beside them, men and women.

My breath catches at the final entry.

President: William Stratford

Proof that he was in the Shakespeare Society. Proof that he was in charge of it while he was a student here. But that doesn't mean he's the one who started it back up. Or that he's in league with them now. No, of course not. I'm being paranoid.

That's what this is. I have some secondhand PTSD from what happened to Daisy.

It's making me see shadows where there aren't any.

Another box contains a stack of thick black cardstock, the same kind he tore up in his office. The same kind that was used for the invitation to the Shakespeare Society. They're a deep dark, not faded or dusty like the other box. They seem new. There are no words on it. No *welcome, students of infinite jest, of most excellent fancy.* No proof of anything, but it's suspicious, at the very least. What would Dean Morris say if he saw this?

"Find anything interesting?" comes a dark voice.

I whirl, clutching the leather binder to my chest. "No."

"No? Then perhaps you ought to put that back where you found it."

"I know who you are."

Two dark eyebrows rise. His T-shirt covers his ridged abs and the beautiful, terrible tattoo, but the image is burned into my mind. "And who's that?"

"You're the one who ran the society. The society that's hurting students like Daisy. You said you were at the masquerade ball to protect us, but that's not true."

I expect him to deny it, but he doesn't. Instead he looks fierce and proud, as dark and glittering as the stranger at the hotel that long-ago night. "That's right."

A sob breaks free. "So you admit it?"

"I admit to fucking you, several times. And I enjoyed each time very much. Not many people claim that those are the actions of a responsible, caring professor. No, I have no claim to honor or integrity. I'm everything you think I am."

I hold up the leather binder. "Are you running the society now?"

"Ah," he says with a faint smile. It's the same smile he used in class when someone said something especially clever. Except now I know I wasn't clever at all. I didn't know who he was until it was too late. Until Daisy was almost hurt. *Until I fell for him.* It's a cruel smile, I can see now. A mocking smile. "Our little mission to make Tanglewood University a better place. That's where I met Arabella, did you know that?"

"No."

He runs his fingertips along my arm. "I thought I was invincible. And then it all fell apart. It got out of control. Arabella ended up pregnant. The school administration in an uproar. The irony is that I didn't even fuck her, but I had to pay the price."

"Brandon isn't yours?"

"He's my son in every way that matters."

"But not blood," I say, swallowing hard.

"I blamed the society for ending up married, for ending up with a baby that wasn't mine. But it wasn't the secret society that did that. It was regular society, with their antiquated rules and puritan beliefs and tedious plodding."

"I don't understand."

He raises an eyebrow. "I thought you were smarter than that. I was mistaken."

Tears threaten, but I fight them back. *I never cry.* "You lied to me."

"I *taught* you. Isn't that what my job is? I taught you how to take a fucking like a good girl, how to bend over and accept what's coming to her, how to get on your knees and suck."

Humiliation rushes over me in waves. "I despise you."

"Do you? Interesting, I suppose. Because I don't feel a single thing for you. Except a slight annoyance that you're in my home."

I've never cried, not for years. Not when my father slapped me or when I woke up covered in fleas. I never cried, prided myself on it, pushed every angry feeling far down. Except now the tears spill over. They drip down my cheeks. He's broken me.

"Why are you doing this?" I ask, my voice ragged.

"I warned you, didn't I? Warned you to stay away from me, away from the Shakespeare Society, tore up your invitation, but you don't listen. Always too damned curious for your own good. Now you found out the truth, but I don't think you're glad of it, are you?"

"No," I whisper, painfully honest, the tears burning hot on my face.

"Ah, well," he says, almost pitying. A step forward. I take a step back, bumping into the wall of books. He plucks the leather folio from my grasp. "*The instruments of darkness tell us truths.*

Do you know the rest? No. A young, innocent little student. You didn't memorize *Macbeth*. An oversight, that. Because Banquo warns that the truth will betray us."

"You're the one betraying me."

"I ruled this school, do you know that? Every student and every professor knew it."

"That was a long time ago."

"Now that I'm back, I remember how much I enjoyed power."

"But you're leaving."

"Oh, didn't I tell you? I accepted a tenured professorship from Dean Morris." Tenure was created to protect professors in positions of sometimes controversial research. It means he can't be fired. "Which means I'm here to stay. For good."

"You can't do this."

"I warned you away once, but you didn't listen. So this time, I'm not leaving any doubt. You were nothing but a passing phase, a cute little co-ed to pass the time, and now it's over."

I take a step back, his form wavy through my tears.

They run down my cheeks like long, liquid brands. My breath shudders out of me. It turns into a gasp. And then another. I'm breaking apart.

Becoming someone who can be hurt by the world—vulnerable and open. My defenses fully destroyed.

He finally did it. Finally made me cry.

It feels as bad as I thought it would. Worse, really. Like I'm fractured into a million pieces. Like the tears are shards of glass, cutting into my skin. The tears don't stop on the long walk to the dorm. I keep my head down, walking, walking. Climbing the stairwell to the dorm so I can avoid people waiting for the elevator.

Lorelei's door is open. She catches me as I'm going by.

"Hey," she says, her tone sharp. "Do I need to call the cops?"

"No," I gasp, unable to say more.

Thank God. I hate paperwork. That's what I expect her to say. Or something equally scathing. Instead, she pulls me into her room and shuts the door. She guides me to her bed and holds me as I sob. As I cry for a tragic ending that everyone saw coming, even me. Especially me. I cry because sometimes foresight isn't a gift. It's a curse.

CHAPTER TWENTY-SEVEN

Cat and Mouse

G RADES SHOW UP next week on our digital transcripts.

However, many professors will post our final grades on printed pages stapled to the wall outside the classrooms. That's where I find myself on the last day of the semester. Every muscle in my body is clenched against the idea of seeing him again. But I already checked my other grades. All As. This is the only one left. It's also the most uncertain.

Not only for me. Everyone is unsure about their grades, considering we didn't get the grades on our essays back. And we aren't sure how he's judging participation.

A few people huddle around the list, some I recognize from my class, some who must be in other classes he taught. I hold my breath as I scan the names.

There are grades listed beside them, many in the 80s, a little less in the 90s.

A handful of 70s. And only one that's failing, at least on first glance.

A. Hall – 100

My breath catches. It's the only 100 on the freaking sheet.

Exhilaration makes my heart beat faster.

Will people be suspicious about why I got a better grade than anyone else? Will they wonder if we had a relationship? Will they question whether I paid in sexual favors?

Don't be silly.

It's not vain to admit that I usually get good grades.

Maybe even the best in the class.

I guess the bigger question is why would he give me such a good grade?

He seemed so angry only a few nights ago.

"Eighty-nine," someone says on their phone as they move away from the paper. "As if it would have killed him to give me the extra point."

I cringe in sympathy, because when converted to a GPA, it will show up as a 3.0 instead of a 4.0, bringing down their average.

345

Only when they move do I see the small table that's piled high with papers.

Our graded essays.

I flip through the list, pausing to smile when I see Tyler's paper title *A Cat and Mouse Courtship*. If I weren't trembling slightly, I might pause and read it for fun. A thick red Sharpie has written *original and subversive!* in slanted handwriting across the top, along with a *95*.

Then I find mine, titled *Cry Me a River*.

The number *100* is scrawled in that same red Sharpie.

No notes, says the only other text.

I stare at the letters for too long, as if hoping they might re-form into something more…expressive. What does that mean? It could mean *no notes because I have nothing to say to you*. Or it could mean *no notes*, in the modern slang way of saying something is perfect.

"Nice," someone murmurs to me, glancing over before rifling through the stack for their own paper.

"Thanks," I say through numb lips.

Then I'm heading back into the sunlight, which feels overbright compared to my mood. The campus bustles with a different energy than it does during classes. People seem lighter, more playful. Many of them carry duffel bags or roll carry-ons as they move out of dorms. We get to keep the same room throughout the academic year, which means any larger furniture or décor can stay. But we won't have access to the building. We can't stay here.

The tiny dorm room feels cavernous without Daisy.

I pack my bags quickly, tossing a couple changes of clothes into my messenger bag. I'm leaving almost everything here, not that I actually have much. I already sold back most of my books to the university bookstore—for a fraction of what I paid, of course.

The campus line takes me to the bus station, where I board the one heading to Port Lavaca. The glass of the window is cool against my forehead. I suppose I should be relieved. I got another 4.0 on a heavy course load. My scholarship is secure. I even had a glimpse, however short, however terrible, of what it felt like to belong somewhere.

My phone buzzes, and I whip it out.

I've been texting Daisy every day, but I haven't gotten anything back.

I'm not even sure she still has her phone.

But it's not her. Instead it's an email from the

dean's office, similar to the one that asked me to spy for them. Except this one has an official-looking letterhead image at the top.

We are pleased to inform you that you have been named to the dean's list.

It's signed by Dean Morris with congratulations for my academic achievements.

It's everything I wanted, everything I worked for, even if I may have lost my best friend. Even if I have to go back to a home of filth and lies. Even if I lost the man who made me feel like a woman. After all, I never really had him. He was never mine.

Thank you for reading THE PROFESSOR! Find out what happens next semester when Anne returns to Tanglewood University—and Professor Stratford is her faculty advisor...

William Stratford is more than my professor.

He's my one-night stand. My secret. And my enemy.

I have a plan for fighting him, along with the secret society that threatens the college. Despite his knowledge and his power, despite the sensual thrall he holds over me, when the bell rings, he's the one who's going to learn a lesson.

At least that's the plan.

But Professor Stratford is older and wiser.

He makes the rules, and I'm forced to follow them.

Want to read Professor Avery Miller's story? She has her own steamy story!

The price of survival...

Gabriel Miller swept into my life like a storm.

He tore down my father with cold retribution, leaving him penniless in a hospital bed. I quit my private all-girls college to take care of the only family I have left.

There's one way to save our house, one thing I have left of value.

My virginity.

A forbidden auction...

Gabriel appears at every turn. He seems to take pleasure in watching me fall. Other times he's the only kindness in a brutal underworld.

Except he's playing a deeper game than I know. Every move brings us together, every secret rips us apart. And when the final piece is played, only one of us can be left standing.

"Sinfully sexy and darkly beautiful, The Pawn will play games with your heart and leave you craving more!"

– Laura Kaye, New York Times bestselling author

Sign up for the VIP Reader List to get free books, bonus scenes, and find out when my books go on sale:

www.skyewarren.com/newsletter

I appreciate your help in spreading the word, including telling a friend. Reviews help readers find books! Please leave a review on your favorite book site.

You can also join my Facebook group, Skye Warren's Dark Room, for exclusive giveaways and sneak peeks of future books.

Keep reading for an excerpt from THE PAWN...

ONE THICK EYEBROW rises. "What do you want with him?"

A sense of familiarity fills the space between us even though I know we haven't met. This man is a stranger, but he looks at me as if he wants to know me. He looks at me as if he already does. There's an intensity to his eyes when they sweep over my face, as firm and as telling as a touch.

"I need..." My heart thuds as I think about all the things I need—a rewind button. One person in the city who doesn't hate me by name alone. "I need a loan."

He gives me a slow perusal, from the nervous slide of my tongue along my lips to the high neckline of my clothes. I tried to dress professionally—a black cowl-necked sweater and pencil skirt. His strange amber gaze unbuttons my coat, pulls away the expensive cotton, tears off the fabric of my bra and panties. He sees right through me, and I shiver as a ripple of awareness runs over my skin.

I've met a million men in my life. Shaken hands. Smiled. I've never felt as seen through as I do right now. Never felt like someone has turned me inside out, every dark secret exposed to the harsh light. He sees my weaknesses, and from the cruel set of his mouth, he likes them.

His lids lower. "And what do you have for collateral?"

Nothing except my word. That wouldn't be worth anything if he knew my name. I swallow past the lump in my throat. "I don't know."

Nothing.

He takes a step forward, and suddenly I'm

crowded against the brick wall beside the door, his large body blocking out the warm light from inside. He feels like a furnace in front of me, the heat of him in sharp contrast to the cold brick at my back. "What's your name, girl?"

The word *girl* is a slap in the face. I force myself not to flinch, but it's hard. Everything about him overwhelms me—his size, his low voice. "I'll tell Mr. Scott my name."

In the shadowed space between us, his smile spreads, white and taunting. The pleasure that lights his strange yellow eyes is almost sensual, as if I caressed him. "You'll have to get past me."

My heart thuds. He likes that I'm challenging him, and God, that's even worse. What if I've already failed? I'm free-falling, tumbling, turning over without a single hope to anchor me. Where will I go if he turns me away? What will happen to my father?

"Let me go," I whisper, but my hope fades fast.

His eyes flash with warning. "Little Avery James, all grown up."

A small gasp resounds in the space between us. He already knows my name. That means he knows who my father is. He knows what he's done. Denials rush to my throat, pleas for understanding. The hard set of his eyes, the broad strength of his shoulders tells me I won't find any mercy here.

Want to read more? Find THE PAWN at Amazon, Apple Books, and other bookstores!

Books by Skye Warren

Endgame Trilogy & more books in Tanglewood

The Pawn

The Knight

The Castle

The King

The Queen

Escort

Survival of the Richest

The Evolution of Man

Mating Theory

The Bishop

North Security Trilogy & more North brothers

Overture

Concerto

Sonata

Audition

Diamond in the Rough

Silver Lining

Gold Mine

Finale

Rochester Trilogy & more
Private Property
Strict Confidence
Best Kept Secret
Hiding Places
Behind Closed Doors

Chicago Underground series
Rough
Hard
Fierce
Wild
Dirty
Secret
Sweet
Deep

Stripped series
Tough Love
Love the Way You Lie
Better When It Hurts
Even Better
Pretty When You Cry
Caught for Christmas

Hold You Against Me
To the Ends of the Earth

The Modern Fairy Tale Duet
Beauty and the Professor
Falling for the Beast

For a complete listing of Skye Warren books, visit
www.skyewarren.com/books

About the Author

Skye Warren is the bestselling author of dangerous romance such as the Endgame trilogy. Her books have been on the New York Times, the USA Today, and the Wall Street Journal bestseller lists. They feature powerful men and the strong women who bring them to their knees. She makes her home in Texas with her loving family, sweet dogs, and flying squirrel.

Sign up for Skye's newsletter:
skyewarren.com/newsletter

Like Skye Warren on Facebook:
facebook.com/skyewarren

Join Skye Warren's Dark Room reader group:
skyewarren.com/darkroom

Follow Skye Warren on Instagram:
instagram.com/skyewarrenbooks

Visit Skye's website for her current booklist:
skyewarren.com/books

COPYRIGHT

This is a work of fiction. Any resemblance to actual persons, living or dead, business establishments, events or locales is entirely coincidental. All rights reserved. Except for use in a review, the reproduction or use of this work in any part is forbidden without the express written permission of the author.